LASTING LOVE

LASTING LOVE

•

Tara Randel

AVALON BOOKS
NEW YORK

PRINTED IN THE UNITED STATES OF AMERICA
ON ACID-FREE PAPER
BY HADDON CRAFTSMEN, BLOOMSBURG, PENNSYLVANIA

To Randy—for your continuous support and encouragement.
I love you.
And to Kimberly Llewellyn—more than a critique partner,
a true friend.

Acknowledgments

A very special thank you to: Debby Mayne, for her encouragement and faith, to Paula Decker for her insight and suggestions, to Megan and Kathryn for your patience, to Mom and Dad for always being there, to Jeanie and Ann for great bouncing sessions, to Dawn and Robin for many prayers, and yes, Holly, country music is about life.

Chapter One

Casey Hudson stepped from the shade of the towering oak tree into the late June sunlight. Her gaze settled on the white two-story farmhouse. "I don't know."

"As I mentioned, it's been vacant for about a year," the real estate agent reminded her, pouring on the sales pitch. "The renovations were never finished, but besides that, I'm sure you'll find the house is just what you've dreamed of."

Casey clutched her purse tighter and started up the sidewalk to the porch. Despite her initial reservations, she couldn't ignore the excitement in her heart.

After fifteen years, she was coming home. She wanted this to be her dream house. "Can you call the contractor? Maybe he'll consider finishing the job for me."

"I'll get in touch with him right away," the Realtor

1

said, falling into step next to Casey. "Hold on, let me find the key to the lockbox."

Casey slowly climbed the three steps to the wrap-around porch. Her fingers brushed over the aging wood and a shiver skirted down her arm. She closed her eyes for a moment, drinking in the stillness of her surroundings, inhaling the fresh fragrance of blooming flowers and summer. Here, in the Blue Ridge Mountains of north Georgia, she would fulfill her dream while coming to terms with her past.

She'd started a craft consignment business with her cousin, and with a rumor of competition closing in, her plans for expansion were already in the works. She'd make a mark for herself and be proud of what she accomplished. No father giving her unwanted advice, no boss stealing her ideas. This time, she was on her own.

Casey stepped over the threshold and her breath caught in her throat. Dust motes danced over the pine plank floorboards, caught in the sunlight from an etched oval window placed at the midpoint of the winding staircase. "Wow."

A breeze swept through the open door and into the foyer, ushering in air sweetened by the new summer grass, along with the fervent hope that this could become her home.

This house wouldn't have the cold, uniform style of a contemporary high-rise. Or the empty echoes of the villa. That had been her parents' choice. This would be her home, as warm and cozy as she could make it.

Marilyn Banner arched a calculating brow. "It has promise, and it will only take a few months to finish."

Casey wandered deeper into the living room. A large stone fireplace dominated one wall; the scarred wooden mantel seemed to invite knickknacks, candles, and stockings hung at Christmas. She imagined the potential in this rambling house, and her excitement grew. "What about the barn?"

"It still needs interior work, but once finished, it'll be perfect for your needs."

A smile pulled at Casey's lips. According to her timetable, she'd need to have the barn renovated in time to warehouse the crafts she would showcase in a fall/winter catalog and on her online website. She had the suppliers, artists, and craftspeople; she just needed the space for storage.

"Why would the owners leave the house if they were in the middle of renovations?" she wondered out loud. Her doubts returned. "There's no structural damage, is there?"

"No," Marilyn volleyed back quickly. "You can have an independent inspector check the house if you wish."

"Then what was the problem?" Casey persisted.

"The owner had problems . . . personal ones," Marilyn said. "Come see the kitchen," she invited, her heels echoing on the pine floor as she crossed the room and disappeared through a wide doorway.

Casey followed, stopping short. A big country kitchen greeted her, equipped with new appliances, wooden cabinets, and the feel of home.

As she peeked in the pantry and opened the cupboards, she could picture a large, rowdy family sharing dinners in this room. A husband and children were also a part of her plans, but not in the near future. Not until she met a man who really stole her heart. Then she might be open to the possibility of romance. She didn't want a replay of her last relationship. Miles had used her. He persuaded her to date him, then stole her accounts and gave them to a woman he was seeing while Casey worked out of town. Anger rushed through her. She'd never let that happen again.

"There's plenty of room here for your family and business," Marilyn commented, her tone curious for personal information.

Casey turned from the sink where she was admiring the ivory-handled faucet. "For now, building a business is all the commitment I'm interested in."

Nonplussed, Marilyn continued the hard sell. "The previous owner remodeled the kitchen first."

"It's beautiful." Casey's thoughts came back to the present as she stroked the oak cabinetwork with awe. "Great taste."

"He did manage to get this right," Marilyn drawled.

Casey could tell from the woman's tone that maybe she'd be happy to dish out more dirt. Fifteen years away from this town and things hadn't changed much. Gossip still ruled. And Casey had always avoided it.

She may have been away from Paineville for many years, but memories assailed her at every turn. She thought about those final days before she moved away. Circumstances had spun out of control. Nearly getting arrested for going along with a group prank was the perfect excuse for her parents to drag her away from the town she loved. Now she was back with a vengeance.

Her gaze was drawn to the large window directly over the deep ceramic sink. The warm summer weather had turned the lawn in the rolling backyard a tender shade of green. A gazebo with faded and chipped white paint sat forlornly to the right of the yard. That picture, more than anything else, gripped her heart. Why, she didn't know. Maybe she felt a kinship to the run-down structure. She shook her head. Now she was getting maudlin.

She had made her decision and she'd stick by it.

"If you're pleased with what you see, let's return to the office and I'll start the paperwork."

Casey tapped her finger against her lip, discreetly observing Marilyn. When they'd been in school, Marilyn had been quiet and subdued, so unlike the savvy professional eager to flesh out the details of a sale.

Casey glanced around the country kitchen and smiled. Now that she felt a kinship with the house, her business mind was already starting to sort through the details. Turning to Marilyn, she said, "Once we close on the deal, I'll move in and get started."

"I can't guarantee I'll find someone to work on the house so soon," Marilyn hedged. "The best builder between here and Atlanta is sort of . . . preoccupied. Maybe you can stay with your cousin a little while longer?"

"No, it's time to leave. Besides, I don't mind a little mess, and I plan on being too busy to notice."

Marilyn nodded and closed her purse, her duty of showing the house over. "Whatever you want."

Casey took one last look around the house, smiling

as she joined Marilyn on the porch. "It's definitely what I want."

Ty Banner took one look at his sister storming up the front steps and wished he'd stayed in Atlanta.

"Were you going to wait till next year to contact me?" Marilyn asked. "I've been calling you for three days. Didn't Gran give you my messages?"

Ty crossed his long legs at the ankles and grinned. Ever since Marilyn had started in the real estate business, she hounded him left and right. Inspect this house. Find a crew to repair that house. He shrugged. She'd always been in a hurry to "be someone," as she put it.

"What is it now? One of Ruby Sue's friends needs a step fixed on her porch?" He grinned. Marilyn shot him a glare which only made him grin wider.

"I hate it when you call Gran by her first name."

"It doesn't bother Ruby Sue."

Marilyn sniffed. "She encourages you. You're like two peas in a pod."

"I wouldn't talk if I were you. We're family, and blood is thicker than water."

Marilyn brushed the seat of the rocking chair before she settled her expensively clad body down. "Forget that. I have good news. I just sold the old Winston farmhouse."

His fingers tightened around the arm of the rocker. He hated that house and everything he'd hoped his future would hold when he'd bought it. "Great."

Marilyn waited a beat, then continued. "You might not think so when you hear the condition of the sale."

"What is it?"

"The buyer wants possession now and the repairs finished within two months."

"No way."

"This is the best offer you'll get. I suggest you take it." Marilyn's tough-sell edge softened. "I know the job wasn't completed because of your problems with Sabrina, but I hoped *you* would finish up the old place."

Ty closed his eyes and rested his head against the wooden back of the rocker. "Who's moving in?"

"Casey Hudson."

Ty opened one lid. He kept his voice even. "Bonnie Owens's cousin?"

"The same. They've started a business together and are quite successful."

He closed his eye and slowly rocked. He hadn't thought of Casey Hudson in years.

"Well?" Marilyn urged. "She wants to move in immediately."

"No can do."

"And why not?"

"I won't be able to find a crew that fast."

He heard his sister expel a frustrated breath and held back his grin. As much as he didn't want to set foot in that house again, he couldn't resist baiting her. She took moving up the ladder of success way too seriously.

"Then do it yourself. The only real work left is to finish the living room, right?"

Ty nodded.

"And then there's the barn renovation. If you can

find a good crew for that it'll take what, two months tops?"

Ty's stomach clenched. His lack of a crew apparently fell on deaf ears. On top of that, Marilyn was being fatally optimistic. If he started now, that would bring them to the end of August. He'd finish all right, because he didn't plan on being around after that.

"Same conditions as before?" he asked, picking up the conversation where they had left off.

"Yes. Casey's already started moving, but you can start immediately."

"Can't. Ruby Sue needs me to, uh, weed the garden."

Marilyn rose, setting the chair to rocking wildly. Ty finally looked at her, noting the teasing glimmer in her eyes. "Nice try. Gran would skin you alive before she'd let you touch her precious garden, weeds or no weeds. And I need this sale to get my picture in the office window as employee-of-the-month. Please, do this for me?"

Ty rolled his eyes at her pitiful ploy to get him working. She went for the jugular when he didn't respond the way she wanted.

"Besides," she began, "you can't use Gran as an excuse for not going on with your life."

He leaned forward, resting his elbows on his knees. "I came home to help out Ruby Sue. I've made sure she's been to the doctor, just like you asked. So now, you can hire me out for a job, but stay out of my personal life."

He sighed. God how he hated this conversation, but

he knew in the end he'd help his sister. "I'll be out tomorrow morning."

"Thanks." Marilyn bent down as if to kiss his cheek, then abruptly stepped back. "I appreciate it."

Ty didn't.

And he didn't think Casey Hudson would either.

"Ty Banner?"

Ty placed his toolbox onto a drop cloth protecting the pine floor. "Yep." He looked across the room and saw the woman who went with the voice.

He did a double take. Little Casey had grown up. She'd lost that adolescent awkwardness he'd remembered so vividly. Her slender frame looked terrific in a calf-length skirt and silky blouse. He quickly lowered his eyes, but not before her wide-eyed stare sent his blood pressure soaring.

"Marilyn didn't tell me you were the contractor."

"Sorry to disappoint you."

Surprise lit her features. "It's not that. I wouldn't have thought you'd come if you knew I bought the place."

"Marilyn is persuasive."

Casey narrowed her eyes, viewing him more intently. He couldn't help but notice the flare of interest that flashed there. "I guess I remembered you and Marilyn looking more alike."

"If my sister let her hair go back to her natural shade, the resemblance would be unmistakable."

"Oh."

He turned his back to her, trying to collect his thoughts before deciding where to start working. In tne back of his mind, he warned himself not to make the usual comparisons to Sabrina. He was here to work, not to size up Casey Hudson.

"Would you like some coffee?" she asked, as she headed into the kitchen.

"Thanks." He laid down the tools and reluctantly followed her into the kitchen. He opened his mouth as he entered the room, stopping short at the scene before him.

Casey stood a few feet away from the counter, a stream of bright morning sunlight cascading in from the window behind her. In that light, he noticed the bright highlights in her honey brown–colored hair. What a picture of femininity she made, from the top of her head all the way to the tips of her toes. Bare toes at that. With toenails painted bright pink. He couldn't take his eyes off her.

"It's all yours," she said.

"Excuse me?"

She tilted her head and held out a mug. "The coffee."

He accepted the steaming coffee cup from her hand. As her fingers brushed his, he felt their softness. Felt a fleeting jolt of pleasure. He immediately hardened his heart.

Casey drew back her hand and curled a lock of hair behind her ear. As he swallowed the steaming coffee, he remembered the last summer they'd spent together. She'd grown up physically since then—so much so it was all he could do to keep from gaping. And imagining. He nearly choked on the hot liquid.

"Are you okay?" she asked with concern.

"Just fine," he muttered. Where had all these ┊ical jolts come from?

He blinked and stared at her innocent face as ᴗne continued to watch him with a tentative smile. Dimples formed in a fresh and clean complexion, and his fingertips ached to touch her face. He gripped the cup handle tighter to keep his hands to himself, and regarded the rest of her.

Her eyes were darker than her wavy hair, a rich chocolate shade. Her feminine body curved and dipped in all the right places, hidden beneath stylish clothes. All in all, a very attractive package on the surface. But who knew what lay hidden beneath the appealing exterior?

He was determined to stay firm in his resolve not to get involved with women. They only spelled trouble and a broken heart.

"I should get to work." He stumbled over his words in his haste to get away from the confusing barrage of thoughts that was giving him a headache.

"Right. Me, too." She grabbed her mug and disappeared into the dining room while he ventured back into the living room.

He gazed down into the dark brew and his mind went blank for a moment. Until he realized that Casey's eyes matched the color of the rich coffee. He thought back to the image of her in the kitchen, her hair gleaming in the sunlight. He closed his eyes and her smiling face materialized before him. Man, what had he gotten into?

He also recalled the intense flare of interest that had swept over her face. It was unmistakable.

He set the mug on the fireplace hearth and ran his palms over his eyes. What was wrong with him? He hadn't even looked at a woman in almost a year. And now, with Casey, he couldn't stop thinking about her.

He forced his thoughts to the task at hand, searching his memory to remember just where he'd left off and what needed to be done to the house. In its original state, it had a small parlor that connected to the dining room at the front of the house and the kitchen at the rear. A moderate-sized bedroom lay directly behind the parlor, so the plan was to rip out the wall and make one big, cozy living room. Before leaving, Ty's crew had begun removing the wall, but then work had abruptly halted.

He stared blindly at the partial opening, unwanted memories assaulting him.

From down the hall, Casey called, "Do you know anything about computers?"

Her voice embraced his senses and he shook his head to clear away the past. "A little," he called back, not daring to take one step in her direction. *Coward,* his inner voice scorned.

She appeared around the corner, her skirt swirling around trim calves. "Enough to set up a new system fresh out the box?"

"Afraid not."

She sighed. "Guess I should have set up an appointment with a tech to do this." She leaned against the door frame. "Are you *sure* you're Marilyn's brother?"

"Positive."

"Hmm." Casey regarded Ty from across the length of the room, sure that fate was playing a game on her.

Elegant, well-dressed Marilyn Banner could not be related to this rugged, disheveled contractor.

As much as she tried not to believe it, the proof stood before her. Fifteen years ago she'd had a major crush on the guy. They met in the school library when Ty asked her to help him with an English report. Their friendship began right then. They had met daily until he finished the report. Too soon, the school year ended and Ty graduated, but he'd surprised Casey by calling her.

He'd been interested in her, she was sure of it. When she thought about the last night she'd seen him, the same night he kissed her, her face grew hot. He'd warned her not to take off with her troublemaking friends, but she hadn't listened. She had borrowed trouble instead.

So now here she stood, face to face with her childhood daydreams. He seemed so unapproachable now.

Shaking off the memories, Casey tried to reconcile the young boy to the present Ty. He wore old jeans with holes in the knees. The equally worn denim shirt had such permanent wrinkles, she wondered if he slept in it and rolled out of bed this morning to come directly to work. She couldn't tell the condition of the black T-shirt underneath, but she could imagine its state of wear.

No, this had to be a mistake. The Ty she remembered was full of life, full of games, on the edge. The man before her had the worn look of a man over the edge. Eyes didn't lie. His held a soul-deep sadness.

While not the same shade as his sisters, his blue eyes had the same shape, and both had the same dis-

...active cheekbones. His jet-black hair was at odds with his sister's blonde, but hers obviously came from a bottle.

The more she examined him, the more the resemblance became obvious; from the overly confident slant of his chin to the way his brows angled when thinking. The longer she scrutinized him, the stronger her reluctance grew to bring up the past with him.

Despite his untidy appearance, he was still very good-looking. Just what she needed, a summer cooped up with a gorgeous slob.

"Seen enough?" he asked in a wry tone.

"Yes. I see the resemblance." *Good save,* she thought to herself, even though she was sure he saw through her bluff.

"Yeah, well, don't let it fool you. We aren't that much alike."

She glanced at his rumpled clothing. "Now *that* I believe."

She smiled, then turned on her heel and returned to the melee of computer components scattered on her dining room table. Her spirits plummeted, and with a sigh, she trudged into the kitchen to use the phone. She sucked in a breath when she noticed the slight tremor in her hand. She wasn't that upset about the computer. Surely the man in the next room hadn't caused this trembling.

She tiptoed to the doorway and peeked into the living room. Absorbed in his work, he didn't notice her. Good. She didn't want him to think she was staring at him. She just couldn't help herself. He was too messy and too darn good-looking not to sneak another look.

Silently chastising herself for spying, she switched her mind to the task at hand: making the phone call. She had just started pressing the buttons when Ty sauntered into the room. She jumped, feeling absurdly guilty.

And utterly fascinated.

Holding up his mug, he poured coffee from the pot. "Takes a couple to get me going."

Casey heard a busy signal and replaced the receiver. "Help yourself. I'll make more if you need it."

"Thanks." He leaned back against the counter.

Suddenly at a loss for words, Casey felt the room shrink and her temperature rise.

"Sorry I can't help you with the computer." Ty nodded toward the dining room.

"It's my fault. I should have made arrangements." She crossed her arms, suddenly self-conscious at being alone with Ty. The silence made her restless. Or maybe it was the man.

All the while she felt Ty's steady gaze on her. Tucking her hair behind her ear, she decided to take a stab at conversation. "So, I understand you originally headed this project."

"Yep." He took a sip of coffee.

She cleared her throat. "Your sister said the owner had personal problems so the work stopped."

"Well, that's what happens when a woman cheats on her fiancé. Lives change."

She noticed an abrupt shift in his mood. Growing wary, she focused on Ty's closed expression. "Did you know them?"

His tortured blue eyes boldly met hers. "She was engaged to me."

Casey nearly lost her breath at his announcement. She hadn't known. That would teach her to listen more closely to local gossip. "I'm sorry. I didn't realize. . . ."

Pushing away from the counter, Ty closed the space between them. Her breath caught in her throat as he loomed over her. "That's okay." He stared at her with a critical frown. "This time."

"So this was *your* house?"

"At one time."

"But your sister called it the old Winston place."

"Old names stick around here."

She stared up at him, her heart going out to him. "You must be uncomf—"

His face closed in on hers. She felt his warm breath fan over her face. Her heart pounded. "Let's make some ground rules."

She swallowed "Okay."

"First, no mention of my ex-fiancée. I don't talk about her to anyone. Ever."

She nodded. "Fair enough."

"And let's keep this thing between us on a professional basis."

"What thing?" she asked, confused at his change in topic.

"Don't tell me you haven't noticed that old attraction between us."

She met his glare head-on. Of course she was attracted to him—what female wouldn't be? "Look, let's not get carried away here. It's been a long time." She broke off, all too aware of the heat in his eyes, the unsteadiness of his breathing.

This could be trouble. Big trouble.

She lifted her chin. "You're here to finish a job and I have my own work to do. I can be just as impersonal as the next person."

"Ditto."

After a few charged seconds of exchanged glares, Ty stalked into the living room and Casey sagged against the wall, expelling a pent-up breath.

This was going to be a long, hot summer.

Chapter Two

"Are we talking about the same guy?" Casey's cousin, Bonnie Owens, stared at her in disbelief.

"Haven't you been listening to me?" Casey fumed, straightening a display rack. Like she'd make this story up.

"Yeah," Bonnie snickered, "and I've been trying to imagine Ty as you described him."

"Have you ever known me to exaggerate?" The aromatic scent of candles and potpourri surrounded her as she worked.

"Hmm." Bonnie tapped a pencil on the counter. "There was that time—"

"Never mind." Casey grinned and grabbed another invoice from the pile on the counter. She cautiously pulled the corner of one paper stuck under a standing display, careful not to topple the wooden key chains. "Any luck finding Mrs. Gibson?"

Bonnie Owens shook her head and a springy mop of auburn curls tumbled around the shoulders of her bright yellow blouse. She'd been Casey's best friend and confidante since they were children, and Casey loved her like a sister. "She's still away visiting."

"I don't know how that woman stays in business. Since I've been here she's had her antique store open three weeks, then she left again."

"Case, you're not in corporate America anymore. You forget what it's like. People put out 'gone fishin' signs all the time. Mrs. G will be back in time for the season. Things always work out."

Doodling a note on the corner of the invoice, Casey shook her head. She'd lived in the small town of Paineville, named after the most prominent family in the county, until she was fifteen. She started hanging around with a fast crowd and had gotten into trouble, so her father had requested a transfer and they'd left for good. Back now for six months, she desperately wanted to fit in. She fervently hoped things would work out this time.

But the slow pace was at odds with her views of business. If it hadn't been for Bonnie and the fact that she'd lived here for years, it would have taken longer to find enough craftspeople to fill her consignment shop.

They'd settled into a profitable cycle, only to learn that major competition might be headed their way. It wasn't surprising. Tourists had discovered Paineville, with its charming old-town flavor and proximity to campgrounds, restored inns, and beautiful mountains and state parks. Anyone with an entrepreneurial spirit could see the potential.

But it worried her. All her savings had gone into this venture. Not to mention her heart and soul. She'd hate to lose any of the momentum she'd built to a competitor.

"Oh, by the way," Bonnie said, "I found another wood carver to add to the inventory. His name is Mike Post. He's well-known around here and up into the Carolinas. He wants to travel less but sell more."

"Mike Post? Why does that name sound familiar?"

"He was Ty's best friend in high school."

"That's right. I remember he kept Ty out of trouble."

"When I spoke to him, he liked our marketing strategy, especially with your new online catalog idea."

"What's not to like? We do the selling and let the artists do the creating. Bottom line, more income for all of us."

Bonnie grinned and the curls bounced again. "We all like that."

Casey smiled and went back to the invoices and calculator. It was still too early to open the store, so they'd met to go over inventory, pricing, and receipts.

The atmosphere created a homey feeling, unlike the staid offices she'd worked in before. She looked up at the rows of crafts, artwork, and wood carvings that made up Crafty Creations. The idea for the shop had played in her mind for years, but it wasn't until she had mentioned the idea to Bonnie last year that it seemed possible.

Bonnie's two children were in school and she

wanted to do something away from the house. She knew the craftspeople in the area and had a knack for the trade. Bonnie's strengths complimented Casey's. Before they knew it, a business was born.

The picturesque town square with two-story Victorian storefronts drew folks searching for a glimpse into simpler times. The homey craft store had quickly been embraced. They ran the store for the first few months and, surprised by the quickness of their success, Casey had decided to move into phase two: online and catalog sales. Especially if she wanted a head start over the possible competition. And for that, she needed her own home. Which led her to the old Winston place.

And Ty Banner.

Bonnie slipped off her stool and bent to remove several cross-stitch packages from a box. "So, run this story about Ty by me again. I'm still having trouble picturing him setting foot into that house."

Casey felt her cheeks heat up as she remembered their last conversation. She'd really put her foot in her mouth. She'd successfully avoided him in the last day or two, hadn't even spoken to Ty, but knew she would eventually. For the past few mornings, Casey left a pot of coffee on for him, then left him alone.

"He really doesn't like being there, but promised his sister he'd finish the job." She grabbed a hanger and hung up one of the white cotton appliqué shirts sold in the store.

Bonnie walked over to the display wall. "He'd promise her anything. They're thicker'n thieves."

Casey held her tongue, knowing better than to point out to her cousin the danger of judging others. She'd broken her cardinal rule of not getting involved in other people's troubles when she made her personal comment to Ty, and ended up with him angry at her for it.

"I have to admit," Bonnie continued, "I haven't seen Ty around much. No one has. Guess the breakup took its toll."

Casey groaned and dropped her head in her hands.

Twirling around at the sound, Bonnie hurried back to the counter, her eyes narrowed suspiciously. "What are you groaning about?"

Separating her fingers, Casey peeked out. "I didn't know he owned the house and I mentioned the breakup."

"Whoa." Bonnie took Casey's hand in hers. "When you put your foot in, you do it big time."

"Next time you gossip, I plan to listen. It may save me from any other embarrassing situations."

Bonnie dropped her hands. "I don't gossip. I merely relay information."

"Whatever you call it, I plan to listen."

Bonnie huffed and stomped away, leaving Casey to grin at her cousin's back. Bonnie hated it when the family teased her about her gossiping skills. Her husband, Chuck, affectionately called her Snoop.

"Besides," Bonnie justified, "it's good for business. Keeps us on top of things."

Casey chuckled and wondered what Bonnie called it *before* they opened the store.

She breathed a sigh of relief that she'd never told Bonnie much about her past relationship with Ty; how they'd met in the high school library or that one balmy

July night when they sat behind the general store in the dim light of the back porch alley and talked for hours. It was a night sweet teenage dreams were made of.

When Casey insisted she leave with her friends, Ty had tried every argument to make her go home. She'd been so cocky, sure the prank to break into the general store was no big deal. He'd looked at her like the foolish fifteen-year-old she was, and walked away. She hadn't seen him again.

The years had passed and now Casey found herself wondering what, besides his obvious dislike of her, made a handsome hunk like Ty so uptight about their renewed attraction. And she had to admit, her curiosity was aroused big time. She wanted to get to know Ty better, just as she was beginning to that summer before she moved. After minutes of Bonnie's silence, Casey broke down.

"Okay, so tell me about Ty. I should be prepared. He's spent nearly a week working, and other than our conversation the first day, I don't know a thing about what happened to him after I left."

Bonnie rushed up from the back of the store, a flush covering her freckled cheeks. "I thought you'd never ask."

She slid back onto the stool and took an indulgent sip of coffee. "Remember Sabrina Post from junior high? Miss Paine County, three years running?"

Sabrina. "Yes. I remember." Figures Ty would be involved with a beautiful woman. "Wait a minute. Mike's sister?"

"Yep. She met up with Ty at some party a few years

back and they got engaged lightning quick. Mike tried to keep Ty from rushing headlong in, but Ty had just been offered a partnership in Atlanta and Sabrina begged him to take it. The guys had a falling out and then Ty refused a big local contract to build resorts around here so they could move. He made a fortune remodeling businesses the year before the Olympics."

Casey looped her finger into the handle of her mug. "What happened with the local resort?"

"At first no one took it up, which upset the locals. It was a chance to give jobs to quite a few folks. Eventually another firm came in and built Fawn Lake. But I think the townsfolk never got over Ty's desertion."

"Why didn't Mike want Ty involved with his sister? I mean, what could be better, your best friend marrying into the family."

"It was no secret that Mike and Sabrina didn't get along. They're so different, it's hard to believe they're related. Mike had no illusions about what his sister wanted: money. Guess he didn't want Ty to be a casualty of Sabrina's greed."

"That makes sense." It also explained Ty's refusal to discuss the past. Casey's heart went out to him. She understood betrayal all too well. She'd pulled herself together, gone on with her life, and hoped Ty would do the same.

Bonnie took another long sip, her eyes alight, relishing in the drama of the story. "Then, a few months ago, Ty came home. Alone. All anyone heard was that he'd split from Sabrina. Ty won't talk, and his family is just as tight-lipped. They always were a tight bunch."

"You make that sound like a bad thing."

Bonnie fumed. "I know how you feel about butting into other people's business. But Case, how do you expect to learn anything if you don't listen to others?"

In a weird way, she made sense.

Casey rubbed the back of her neck. "So when you come right down to it, you don't know what happened."

Bonnie pouted. "I know enough." She slid from the stool, grabbing an open box of tags, and crossed the room to a display shelf.

Casey laughed at Bonnie's melodramatics. She'd never been involved in office rumors or politics at her last job, although if she'd paid attention she might have saved herself a big heartache. It wasn't that she didn't have interest, it was just that she'd grown up with people who valued their privacy and Casey considered that a fine trait.

When she'd been the topic of office gossip with Miles, she painfully remembered the humiliation that went with it. So she ignored the pain and went on with her life, hoping others would leave her alone.

Unfortunately, the philosophy was naive.

"I'm sorry, I didn't mean to upset you. You know how much I dislike prying."

Bonnie busied herself separating price tags. "I understand. But let me give you some advice?"

Casey reached into the box and removed more tags. "What kind of advice?"

"Be careful. Ty still isn't over the breakup and he hasn't been too friendly. Don't go around feeling sorry for him. It would be like that fiasco with Miles all over again."

"Miles was a mistake." Casey dropped the tags on the floor near her foot. "And I don't plan on suffering a similar lapse of judgement. Ty Banner and I have only one thing in common—my walls. And my barn. Once he finishes the job, he's history."

Bonnie tried to hide a grave look of concern as she bent down to retrieve the scattered tags. "Good. Getting mixed up with Ty is the last thing you need in your life."

Casey pulled her SUV into the driveway and parked to the side of Ty's battered pickup. Even his truck reflected his personality. She turned off the ignition and stared at the house, her chest filling with excitement as it always did when she viewed it. *My home.*

For years she'd been dragged around with her parents, from one luxurious apartment or townhouse to another. Just as she'd get settled, they'd move again. Her father had never liked small-town life, but stayed because Casey's mom grew up here. After the infamous run-in with the police, her father didn't need much of an excuse to leave. They left Paineville, and shortly after, her father landed a job as an international business broker. From then on they traveled to many famous cities, many exotic locales, but all Casey ever wanted was one home, one place to feel secure. Her father vowed never to return to Paineville now that he'd had a taste of the world, but she'd planned otherwise.

She'd tried the business world, only to be betrayed

by her boss. Miles Sanborn gave her hard-earned sales accounts to a young executive he was dating behind her back, leaving Casey out in the cold. Furious, she quit that day. But Miles's actions were the impetus to get her started on her long-dreamed-of business.

Grabbing the two grocery bags from the passenger seat, Casey exited the car and briskly marched up to the back door. Seeing the top half of the Dutch door open reminded her of Ty's presence. She reached to turn the knob and entered a laundry room adjacent to a small bathroom. The fresh scent of recently cut lumber filled the air. Once in the kitchen, she dropped her bundles on the counter, hearing the steady bang of a hammer.

Trying to ignore the clamor, Casey opened the freezer door and quickly removed a dozen frozen dinners from the bag, sliding them onto the rack. With a slight nudge, she slammed the door shut, turning to the next bag to unpack more staples.

"Mind if I help myself to some ice water?"

Casey swung around, her heart nearly jumping into her throat. She hadn't noticed the hammering had stopped. "Don't sneak up on me like that!"

Ty grinned, crossing his arms over his chest as he rested his shoulder against the door frame. Today he wore a faded plaid shirt with the sleeves torn out over jeans washed so many times that they'd lightened to a soft powder blue. "Sorry. Didn't know you were that jumpy, darlin'."

Darlin'?

Trying to regain her composure, Casey tucked a lock of hair behind her ear and took a breath. "I'm not usually jumpy," she answered defensively. "I thought you were working."

He pushed away from the door frame and sauntered to the sink, passing by her closely. She savored his outdoorsy scent.

"I need ice." He opened the freezer door and turned his head to her, eyes wide. "What's with all the TV dinners?"

She shrugged. "No time to cook."

After getting his ice, he brushed past her again, barely grazing her, then filled the glass with tap water. "I don't have much time either, but even I wouldn't resort to that stuff."

She faced him. "Sometimes when I work I lose track of time. Frozen is easy."

Ty took a long drink, then refilled the glass. He leaned against the counter. And grinned. "You can't cook, can you?"

She stilled. How could he know? "What makes you say that?"

"I've noticed that you never cook anything. You make coffee and sandwiches, but I haven't seen a pot or pan in plain sight."

Casey pulled back her shoulders and faced him squarely. "I've never taken the time to learn. I've just been too busy." She bristled at the twinkle in his eyes. "Besides, it's not the end of the world if I don't cook."

He sighed, setting the glass on the counter and placing a hand over his heart. "It's been so long since I've had a home-cooked meal. A guy can dream."

It took a few seconds for her to realize he was teasing her. All those years of working hard to get ahead took their toll. She couldn't even prepare a decent meal for an attractive man if she wanted to.

"Well," she replied good-naturedly, "you'd better stop at May's Kitchen in town. The only thing I have to offer here is frozen."

He chuckled, resting his palms on the smooth counter surface. For once, he didn't seem in a hurry to return to work. She wasn't about to complain. After all, he hadn't been overly friendly since she arrived and she really did want things to be comfortable between them. But why the change?

"So how does a person get to be, hmm," he perused her from top to bottom, "twenty-five without learning her way around the kitchen?"

Despite herself, Casey smiled. "You're a smooth talker with a bad memory. You're off by six years."

His eyebrow raised in that disarming way she could grow to like. "Thought women never mentioned their real age."

"I don't have a problem with my age. In fact I like where I am in life. So, now that we've established that you're chivalrous, maybe you can explain why you don't make the coffee in the morning."

He shrugged. "You always have it ready when I get here. So, why can't you cook?"

"Tenacious," she muttered under her breath.

"Evasive," he volleyed back.

She walked to the scarred oak kitchen table she had found at a flea market and sat down on a mismatched chair. "We moved a lot after the transfer from here, so my parents hired people to take care of the household. Later, when I moved out on my own, there were

always business dinners or nights out with my friends.
I never had a reason to learn."

"What kind of business did you start out in?"

"I was a buyer for a large company."

"What did you buy?"

She evaded his eyes and traced her finger over a
long scratch on the table surface. "I bought kitchen
goods and housewares for a chain of retail stores."

He burst out laughing.

She tried, unsuccessfully, to glare at him.

"You have to admit, that sure does put a spin on
things."

Deciding to go with the flow, she smiled. "Believe
me, I've heard every joke you can imagine."

He leaned over and said in a loud stage whisper,
"Can you craft anything?"

Instead of being insulted, she went along with his
twenty questions. "Actually, I do some needlework.
So I'm not totally out of the loop at Crafty Creations."

His genuine smile had her stomach flip-flopping. It
felt like old times between them. She recalled that
smile and knew that he didn't share himself that often
anymore. She'd just been treated to a rare occurrence.

Their eyes caught and held for a long minute. Casey
foolishly hoped he'd make an intimate gesture toward
her. A touch. A kiss. Anything to prolong the wonderful agony of their proximity.

Ty blinked, sanity returned, and the moment was
lost.

"I wish you the best of luck." He glanced at his
watch. "I guess I should be getting back to the job."

Casey followed him into the living room. She tried

not to be dismayed by the gaping hole in the wall that seemed to have grown bigger. "What, exactly, are you doing?"

He pulled a tape measure from his metal toolbox and measured a piece of wood end-to-end on saw-horses set a few feet apart. "I've checked the electrical wiring, repaired any damage that came about when we took down the original wall, and now I'm getting ready to build the casing that will finish off the opening."

She stepped closer, curious now. "Don't you have a crew to help you?"

"No, I'm working solo on this one."

By the stony look on his face, Casey got the message that he didn't want to talk anymore. They had already spent too much time together. Casey know more moments like the heated one they'd just shared would lead her into emotional trouble. She didn't come home to catch Ty Banner. She came home to make a secure business for herself. She needed to remember that. "I need to get back to the computer. I'll be in the dining room if you need anything."

Chapter Three

The next morning, Ty set the bag of gourmet coffee on the counter, then rummaged through the kitchen drawers until he found a measuring spoon and filters. The sweet aroma of French vanilla filled the room, along with cheese pastries he'd picked up at the Pastry Palace. He wasn't much for girly coffee, but Casey might like the change.

She hadn't come downstairs yet, although he knew she was awake. They'd formed an unspoken routine. Every morning she left the back door unlocked so he could come in and get going with the job. Today was no different.

He could hear her moving around upstairs. The floors in this old house creaked and grumbled, just like an old man with rheumatism. It was one of the qualities he liked so much when he had bought the house.

He'd been crazy to let Marilyn talk him into taking

this job. Memories of life before Sabrina's betrayal assaulted him daily. Granted, they hadn't actually moved into this house before she betrayed him with his old college roommate and ex-partner, John Rogers.

Sabrina could be very persuasive when she wanted something. Ty had been taken in by her relentless showering of attention, as well as her sophisticated beauty and charm. For a country boy, she was a dream come true.

Until she decided to move on to bigger and better. Ty wanted to return home, to his roots, but Sabrina had it in her mind to stay put in Atlanta. She loved the social life, the elite circle they ran in.

So really, the house hadn't been a part of his and Sabrina's life. He figured it was the emphasis he'd put on his own dreams, dreams that included a house like this, a wife, children. Things that, as a kid, he never thought he'd attain. He'd lost sight of what he originally wanted in his life: acceptance in the community and a successful business. This house triggered those long-buried memories. He figured by now that that constricted sensation would have gone away, but it hadn't.

And he knew when Casey came down those stairs, the band over his diaphragm would squeeze tighter with an entirely different emotion. He grinned. It was a feeling he was getting used to.

"What's that glorious smell?" Casey shuffled into the room, dressed in an oversized T-shirt and baggy shorts. And no shoes to hide her cute feet. This morning her toenails were painted a pale pink.

"Breakfast." Ty discreetly scanned her face, noting

the purplish shadows under her eyes. "Get much sleep last night?"

Casey yawned. "Not really. I started working on the catalog and lost track of time."

She glanced down at her watch. "My gosh, I have to meet Bonnie at the store." She headed for the staircase.

"Freeze." Ty yelled.

She stopped in her tracks and turned to face him, her sweet expression quizzical. "Excuse me?"

He nodded toward the kitchen. "I brought you a present."

Her face lit up and he felt his gut contract. She looked so wide-eyed and innocent this morning without makeup and her hair pulled back in a ponytail, a sight he found vastly appealing. Casey had a natural loveliness that made her beautiful to him.

"What kind of present?" she asked, gingerly stepping over the cord of his electric saw to join him. He couldn't help but admire the sway of her hips. A few strands of tousled hair escaped her ponytail and curled around her face. He found himself wanting to know if she woke up every morning looking this good.

"Are you coming?" She grabbed his hand with sudden impatience and tugged him into the kitchen. He pushed away his wayward thoughts and let her drag him along, purposely forgetting that he didn't want to get involved with any woman. Especially one who stayed up all night and put her business above all else. He'd already been there.

She dropped his hand and opened the pastry box. "Oh," she said and moaned. "My favorite. Of course, this means I'll have to skip lunch, but I'm sure will taste heavenly." She picked up the bag of c and graced him with another appreciative smile. "..y hero."

"Shucks ma'am, you'll set me to blushin'." He unhooked two cups from the mug tree and handed them to Casey. "Since I won't be getting any home-cooked meals in the near future, I figured this would do."

She laughed as she filled the cups to the brim. "Never think the impossible. I might surprise you one of these days."

You already have, he thought. She'd somehow slipped into his thoughts when he was determined to keep her out.

In a few more days he'd be finished in the living room and start on the barn. They wouldn't be in close proximity every day, and then maybe this crazy attraction would pass and he'd get back to normal.

Brooding and alone.

Casey took plates from the cabinet and placed a large, gooey pastry on each. She carried them to the table, then went back for forks. "Since you went to all this trouble, the least we can do is sit down and start the morning with the most important meal of the day."

"I'm sure some would argue with you about that." Ty looked at the empty calories lying in wait. "Big day at the store?"

She took a sip and nodded her head. "We have a large shipment from one of our newest artists arriving today. We put a huge sign up in the window advertising his carving works, so we expect to draw in a lot of regulars. Bonnie says anyone who knows crafts and artwork will be familiar with him and that'll help sales."

"What's his name?"

"Mike Post."

Ty felt a tinge of regret tug at him.

"Weren't you two friends?"

Taking a deep breath, Ty lowered his gaze to the coffee. "He was my best friend. We had a disagreement and haven't kept in contact, but I knew he'd made a name for himself with his work. He's really talented."

He watched her mull that over for a few seconds, obviously putting the name together with Ty's past. Whoever said we all lived in a small world must have come from Paineville, he thought. "So what happened?"

"It's a long story."

"We're having a nice breakfast here. Make conversation."

He felt the darkness lift, and he found himself wanting to tell Casey things he hadn't talked about in years. Just as he'd done when they were teenagers.

"Mike didn't want me to propose to Sabrina. He saw her ambition; I saw her beauty. He thought I should stay here and build homes. Sabrina wanted the big-city life. She won; Mike and I lost touch."

"Now that things have, um, changed, maybe you could get in touch with him."

He frowned. "I don't know. Stupid things were said through the years. He wouldn't want to see me."

Casey reached out and placed her soft hand over his. "But he might."

Ty stared at their hands, the softness versus the roughness. So much like his life. "Or maybe he'd want to gloat and say I told you so."

She laughed and squeezed his hand. The small touch of affection was the most he'd allowed himself to feel in a long time. A very long time.

"If it means you two start talking, it can't be that bad."

He slipped his hand out from under hers. "That's what Ruby Sue tells me. Only she thinks I should talk to everyone I've ever had a difference with. We'll be sittin' around on her front porch at night and she'll start in on me until I have to leave just to drown out her voice. Living with her must be some kind of cosmic punishment."

Casey's eyes grew wide and she dropped her hands in her lap. "Ruby Sue?"

Ty bit his tongue, trying to control his amusement before he explained. Did he notice a flash of jealousy in her eyes? "I'm sorry. I thought you remembered my grandmother."

Casey blinked and sat straighter in the chair. Her voice was tight when she spoke. "Oh."

"Sorry." He chuckled again. "You didn't exactly come from the same neighborhood as us. And I didn't call her by her first name till I got older."

Her righteous indignation turned her cheeks pink. "That may be true, but you still shouldn't speak about your flesh and blood that way."

"You haven't met her."

Silence fell over the room, the only sounds coming from the creak of the house and the birds greeting the morning. Suddenly the joy of the special moment spent with Ty slipped away with Casey's embarrassment. When they first became friends, he had mentioned his unhappy home life. How could she have forgotten the life Ty and his family had lived? His parents had both run off in different directions, leaving behind a broken-hearted young man. His pride had kept him from bringing her to the run-down mobile trailer they'd called home.

He'd spoken so fervently about leaving it behind the night they sat under the starlit sky behind the general store. He'd trusted her by giving her a glimpse of what he saw for his future. How he planned to go to college and get away from the poverty he'd grown up in. That trust had made her first crush a glowing memory. She could never, ever forget that glorious rush of young love.

"So you live with your grandmother?"

"More like on the same property. In the trailer I grew up in. After Marilyn got successful a few years ago, Ruby Sue was alone. Gabe doesn't get home much to help her, so a few years back I built her a house. She's had a couple of falling spells and refuses to see a doctor, so I came back to town. Decided to stay nearby until I figured out what to do with myself."

"Gabe?"

"My brother. His first name is Clark."

"That's right, I remember now." A crazy thought hit her. "What's Ty short for?"

An amusing shade of red ran over Ty's cheeks. "Ty-rone."

"As in Power?"

"My middle name."

"And Clark? As in Gable?"

"His middle name."

"Let me guess. Marilyn's middle name is Monroe?"

Ty ran his hand over the back of his neck. "Yep."

Casey pushed the mug round and round between her hands. She'd never put it all together before. "Do I hear a theme here?"

Ty stood, taking his empty plate and mug to the sink. "My mother loved old movies, had a thing about the old stars." He turned his back to her and leaned against the counter, looking out the window.

"I don't think I ever met your mom."

His shoulders grew stiff and he said in a voice she could barely hear, "She doesn't live around here."

So much for prying, Casey thought. Obviously Ty wanted to keep the past in the past. Who was she to dredge up old memories? She glanced down at the crumbs on her plate and decided she ought to get ready for work. Until Ty turned and pierced her with his compelling gaze.

"Didn't Ruby Sue raise you?" she asked.

He nodded.

Casey smiled, hoping to dispel some of the pain she glimpsed in his eyes. Carrying her plate and mug to the sink, she rinsed them off and tentatively touched his muscular arm, her fingers brushing over the worn cotton of his shirtsleeve. "And she did a fine job. You always were a gentleman. Here I was, a sophomore, awed at the idea of talking to a senior." She laughed. "It seems so long ago."

"Ages." Ty's eyes met hers with a hidden promise

that held her captive. Her mind went blank; she felt like that silly schoolgirl again, lost in the world of an older, worldly upperclassman. The man who'd shared her first kiss.

Casey slowly came to her senses. "So, when will your brother be here? I don't think I've met him, either."

"You'll get to meet him at the Founder's Day parade. He always comes home for that."

"Looking forward to it." She took a step back, needing to leave the room. Quickly. "I've got to get changed. Thanks for the breakfast."

"Anytime."

She hoped he meant it.

Casey arrived at the store to find Bonnie in the back room struggling with the contents of a large box. Another sealed carton waited beside the back door.

"Grab a knife and split the tape," Bonnie instructed. "We received another shipment."

Casey flipped her a jaunty salute. "Yes, ma'am."

"What's put you in such a good mood?" Bonnie asked as she tossed packing material to the floor. "You're nearly a half hour late and when you get off schedule, you usually get hives."

"Go ahead, mock me. Nothing can ruin my good mood."

"Good, because we have a few problems."

Casey put her purse with Bonnie's belongings and picked up the pocket knife from a shelf on the wall. "What kind of problems?"

Bonnie sank to the floor, crossing her legs Indian-style. Like Casey, she'd worn jeans and a signature shirt one of their suppliers showed in the store. "You know how all the shopkeepers in the square are getting ready for Founder's Day?"

"Sure, it's all anyone around here can talk about."

"It's a big deal. Since the Chamber of Commerce helped all the stores rejuvenate the storefronts, we have a very homey town here. Now that it coincides with July Fourth weekend, downtown will be a madhouse with the parade and picnic."

Casey tore open the carton. "The problem?"

"You know those empty stores at the north end of the square? I heard a whisper that Marilyn sold the building."

"That's good for everyone," Casey said, acting casual even as Bonnie's words sent a chill of dread through her. She calmed herself and lifted the lid to start removing the packing.

Bonnie shook her head, sending her unruly curls shaking. "Not if it's a craft shop. Very similar to ours. You know how popular this kind of store is."

Yes, she did. All the research she'd done before opening the store had told her just that. She forgot about the contents of the box and sat down beside her cousin. "We don't know for sure what kind of store will open there."

"Chuck's sister works in the real estate office. She told me about Marilyn's wheeling and dealing. Mentioned something about a chain store. Not only that, but someone is opening an Italian bistro. May over at May's Kitchen is a wreck over the whole thing."

"That shouldn't be a problem. People can get Italian

anywhere. But tourists come here for the down-home ambiance. May won't have to worry."

Tears pooled in Bonnie's eyes. "I hate it when things change."

Casey ran her hand through Bonnie's springy curls. "We knew this would happen when Fawn Lake opened last year. That draws more visitors between here and Atlanta than any other resort. It was bound to happen."

Bonnie sniffed, her face forlorn. "I know, but we're doing so good here."

For the first time since the conversation started, Casey grinned. "Competition is good. It makes us use our brains, be more creative." Her keen business instincts kicked in. "This is where my marketing expertise will come in handy. And I love a good challenge."

Dabbing her eyes, Bonnie started to look hopeful.

Casey jumped up. "Look, it'll take a few months, maybe longer to restore the inside of those buildings. They've been neglected for so long, they'll have to be gutted and completely restored, so new tenants can't move right in. That gives us a head start to come up with even more fresh ideas and work with our artists."

Bonnie pulled herself up. "But what if they leave us?"

"We have to make sure they don't. You know all our suppliers. We'll make sure they don't have a reason to move elsewhere."

Casey walked out of the storeroom and wandered up the aisle to the front door. Her thoughts settled on the impending competition and what it could mean for Crafty Creations. She'd do just fine, she convinced herself. After all, she'd grown to love this place. From the hodgepodge of crafts to the potpourri scent that tickled her nose as soon as she came in the door.

She peered out at the square, to the place she would always think of as home. The Chamber of Commerce offices sat in the middle of the square: a great, red brick building built in the early 1800s. Once a court-house for the county seat, it now housed a museum that celebrated life in this section of the mountains.

As tourists drove into town, they were directed to follow the one-way roads taking traffic along either side of the court house. Along the brick sidewalks tourists strolled beside colorfully decorated storefronts lining the busy square. Window displays attracted attention for the merchants, including mountain wear, antiques, hand-crafted dolls, souvenirs, along with several restaurants like the Victorian Tea Room, May's Kitchen, and the Pastry Palace.

Crafty Creations sat in the center of buildings to the west of the square. The Old General Store operated to the left, the Christmas Nook to the right. At either end was the post office and Kid's Place, a toy and clothing store for children.

All the tenants were friendly, everyone looking out for each other. They were like a big family, one that Casey had come to love since moving here. If Bonnie was so upset about the threat of the new businesses, Casey wondered if the others were as worried and had starting making plans.

"I'm going out," she called to Bonnie and left the shop, heading to the general store. Ben and Molly Pike had run the store all their lives, so Casey knew she'd get the lowdown from them. After they had graciously accepted her apology for the night she and her friends had broken into the store, they'd become good friends.

They'd understood that she had gotten caught up in the prank, that Casey had never meant to hurt them. Nothing had been stolen. One of the boys had picked a lock in the back and they had snuck in, really just to prove they could do it. Unfortunately, they weren't smart enough to stay away from the front window. Someone had called the police and the rest was a blur.

"Hey, stranger," Ben called, as a clanking cowbell over the door announced her entry. As always, the rich aroma of coffee greeted her. Before she could ask, Molly approached her with a steaming cup.

"Where have you been hiding?" Molly asked, as Casey accepted the coffee.

"At home, working on the computer."

Ben, sporting a white bib apron over his comfortably worn clothes, manned the huge, antique cash register behind the counter. "Thought maybe you returned to the big city."

"No way, now that I'm settled in at the old Winston place."

Molly joined her husband. Both had graying hair and glasses, but where Molly was plump, Ben was tall and gangly. And after forty years of marriage, they obviously still adored each other. It gave Casey hope that out there, a special man waited for her.

"You should walk by the real estate office. Marilyn got her picture in the window as salesman of the month for selling that old place to you."

"Salesperson, dear." Molly brushed at a stain on Ben's apron.

"Right." Ben adjusted his glasses. "Anyway, seems your buying the old place did the trick."

"That's true, dear. Marilyn should be proud of her accomplishments."

"Speaking of Marilyn," Casey cut in, "I just found out about the potential sale of the building at the end of the square. What have you heard?"

Molly tsked and started rearranging the old-time stick candy in jars on the counter. She gave more away to children than she actually sold. "Some upstarts from Atlanta. Probably have nothing better to do than come in here and steal business away from us."

"I have to agree." Ben shook his head. "Usually it wouldn't matter none, but the details are being kept as secret as confederate money in a vault."

"It's not like Marilyn to keep things from us, but she's been so evasive lately. I'm wondering if she's having problems with the sale. We don't know what to think." Molly kept moving the jars, a frown wrinkling her forehead.

"Then maybe it's nothing to worry about. It's not like they're planning on building a mall nearby."

Molly gasped. "Dear child, don't say that. Even in jest."

"Sorry." Casey sipped her coffee as her mind worked. This certainly wouldn't be the end of the world. They'd make do.

"So, tell us." Ben rested his elbows on the creaky mahogany counter and leaned toward her. "Heard tell Ty Banner's been working on your place."

"He's finishing some remodeling. Marilyn asked him to do the work."

"Just be careful, dear. He's had a heartbreak and hasn't been himself since he came home."

Casey frowned. "Why should I be careful?"

Molly grinned. "I see that gleam in your eyes when we mention his name."

"Not to mention that blush," Ben added with a chuckle.

"Just take my advice, dear." Molly bustled around the side of the counter, only to stop abruptly. "Come to think of it, I'm surprised Ruby Sue hasn't kicked him out of the trailer by now. It's time he started picking up the pieces of his life." She sniffed. "Ty built the house special for her, but since he's been back, he's holed out in that old trailer. The one the family used to live in. He could stay in that big house with his grandmother if he wanted."

"Molly," Ben interrupted in an authoritative voice. "He's a grown man, been out on his own for years."

"It's the principle," she huffed, reaching for the rotary dial phone mounted on the wall behind them. "I think I'll give Ruby Sue a call."

"You do that. And tell her to give Ty a piece of our mind while you're at it." Ben scowled. "It's not enough that he left to work in Atlanta, giving away that Fawn Lake contract that would have put our local folks to work. No, now he has to bring this trouble on us here. If his granddaddy were alive—"

"Excuse me, what kind of trouble do you mean?" Casey asked.

"Didn't you know? His crew from Atlanta is doing

the remodeling work on those stores we've just been talkin' about. Heard that a national chain store was interested in the place. You know, one of those stores that carries everything for one-stop shopping. With that kind of competition, we're all in trouble."

Casey took an involuntary step back, nearly overturning her coffee, as a sensation like she'd been sucker-punched took her breath away. Blood rushed to her face, along with a strong dose of anger. Was he helping the competition? She tried to mask the resentment in her voice. "He didn't mention it."

"Ty always was one to keep his personal business to himself."

"But this affects the entire town square." She thought about Bonnie's tears, Ben and Molly's concern, and May's fears. How must the other store owners feel?

And to think, she'd trusted him. Told him about her life. He knew the store was important to her, but he'd kept this new information quiet.

Her spirits sank.

She thought Ty was different. But it had been years since she'd known him. People changed. Look at what Miles had done to her. Silently, she renewed her vow not to let anyone stand in the way of her success.

Not even Ty Banner.

"Can't control Ty." Ben shrugged, resigned. "No one's ever been able to."

Casey thought back to the morning, to Ty's good humor, and the fun they'd shared together. A nagging voice urged her to give him the benefit of the doubt. At least until she got to the bottom of things.

But her battered heart warned her not to give him an inch. Or she might be left with less than she had with Miles.

"I know one thing about Ty," Ben cut into her thoughts. "When he makes his mind up about something, not even an earthquake can shake him."

Yeah, well, he hadn't tangled with Casey Hudson yet.

Chapter Four

Casey marched back to Crafty Creations, her mind searching for answers. The fact that Ty had anything to do with remodeling the empty stores bothered her. Not that she expected him to tell her what he was doing; after all, business was business. She could understand that. But she had a nagging sense that something wasn't right.

"Where'd you go?" Bonnie asked, as soon as Casey pulled open the door.

"To talk to Ben and Molly."

The worried frown returned to Bonnie's face. "And they told you the same story. Right?"

"Yes. Except you left out the part about Ty's crew handling the job."

"Get out!" Bonnie paled. "I didn't know that."

Casey examined her cousin. "So fill me in on why

49

we should be concerned about Ty's Atlanta firm handling the job."

Suddenly Bonnie busied herself with rearranging merchandise. "You'll have to ask Ty."

"I plan to. As soon as I get home." Casey headed for the back room, intent on unpacking the delivery. She'd been working for a while before she noticed Bonnie hovering at the door.

"Hey Case, I'm sorry I ruined your good mood this morning."

"No problem." Packing material landed in a heap beside the carton as Casey tossed it out. At the mention of her good morning, she had visions of gooey pastry, French vanilla coffee, and Ty, sitting in her kitchen sharing food and conversation with her.

She pushed those thoughts aside and reminded herself that she was angry with him. No feel-good memories were going to sway her mood.

"So, did something special happen?"

Casey bent into the box. "Yes. I had a breakfast date."

Bonnie tugged Casey upright by the back of her shirt and spun her around. "Please repeat what you said. Your words were muffled so I couldn't have heard that you had company."

Casey grinned slyly. "You heard me."

"Details, girl. Details."

Despite the earlier pall from Bonnie's news, and her renewed vow to keep anyone from ruining her future, Casey felt her pulse quicken. "Ty brought coffee and pastries for me this morning."

Bonnie's jaw dropped.

"We sat at the table and had a nice conversation."

"We're talking about Ty Banner?"

"Why do you always ask me that?" Casey asked, royally annoyed.

"Because it's downright unusual."

Casey slapped her hands onto her hips. "What, that Ty would want to spend time with me?"

"That he'd want to spend time with any woman."

Casey kicked at the material on the floor. "He's been through the ringer emotionally, I could tell that just by talking to him. But he's not so bad off that he can't enjoy my company. Besides, we're just friends. Maybe he needs someone to listen to him."

Casey remembered the fierce expression on his face when Ty said he didn't discuss his past. Yet he'd opened up this morning. Because she hadn't demanded anything more from him than just being a friend.

And in return he kept secrets.

Casey brushed pieces of packing material from her shirt, remembering Ty with sawdust scattered over his worn T-shirt as he worked at the house. His shaggy good looks struck a primal chord within her. His eyes, so dark, so blue, seemed to see inside her, into the compartments no one else knew about.

Silly, she scoffed. She was a healthy red-blooded female, appreciating a good-looking man.

"So, do you plan on breakfasting with him again?" This time Bonnie had that busybody, prying tone to her voice.

"Who knows? Maybe it was a fluke." Casey reached into the box to remove a wrapped carving. "Let's get back to work. We need to get these pieces displayed."

"Slave driver," her cousin muttered, but pitched right in.

By late afternoon, all the pieces had been unwrapped and positioned in the store. A visiting couple from Florida had fallen in love with one wood sculpture of an eagle in descent. Casey had no doubt that this work would sell well. Ty was right, Mike Post had a glorious talent for wood sculpting.

Casey glanced at her watch. "Bonnie, I'm going to head home, maybe get some work done on the computer. Do you mind closing?"

"No problem. Any progress on designing the catalog?"

Casey went to the back to retrieve her purse and stopped by the counter on her way out. "I stayed up all night working. But this project is going to take a while."

"Well, keep at it. Oh, and give Ty my regards."

Casey shut the door on raucous laughter behind her.

Ty wrapped up the cord for his saw, whistling along with a country song on the radio as he loaded up the last of his tools.

He'd hoped to see Casey before he left, but he'd finished the casing around the door and repaired the molding, so there was no reason to hang around any longer today. The only thing left of the job was to connect the flooring at the junction. He knew where to get matching pine and he'd have it installed in no time.

He heard a car door slam just as he closed the toolbox. Sauntering to the kitchen window, he watched

Casey stride up the path. In the late afternoon sun she looked just as lovely as she had this morning. All day he'd been waiting for her to return, yet seeing her now, he felt as though she'd never left.

By the time Casey walked into the living room, Ty had packed up his tools.

"I'm glad you're still here," she started without preamble. "I have something to ask you."

"Go ahead."

"Why didn't you tell us that your Atlanta crew was coming up to restore the empty buildings in the square?"

Her question hit him right in the solar plexus. He inhaled sharply, hoping to mask his surprise. "What're you talking about?"

Casey frowned. "Ben Pike told me your crew was on their way to Paineville. How could you not know?"

That was the question of the hour. But then, he'd deliberately backed out of the loop, so he really didn't know what was going on.

"Did Ben tell you the building was sold?" he asked.

"No. Only that the work would be starting soon. And that a major chain was interested."

In his gut, Ty knew Marilyn was involved. He also realized he'd be having a family heart-to-heart with Marilyn very soon. And if his suspicions were correct, Sabrina's name would soon surface in this mess.

In the meantime, he decided it was best not to involve Casey. It was better that she not work her way any deeper into his life. "Look, not that it's any of your business, but my firm can pick up work anywhere it wants."

Casey's chin lifted. "What about the competition? If this sale affects my store, then it's my business." She walked to the couch that was draped by an old dropcloth when Ty was working, and tossed her purse down. A faint puff of sawdust littered the air. "And some people don't appreciate the fact that locals will miss out on the work."

Ty rubbed his hand over his eyes. The same old song-and-dance. For years his family had been the town joke, three kids left behind by a flighty mother who couldn't be bothered with the mere responsibility of kids, raised by a cantankerous old woman who wouldn't leave the run-down trailer for a decent house. His father couldn't keep a job and walked out when they were babies. No matter Ty's accomplishments, all he got was the long memory of Paineville, a reminder of his family and mistakes.

Now here stood Casey, accusation flaring in her eyes.

"Guess Ben filled you in on Fawn Lake."

Casey tucked her hair behind her ear. "His side of it."

He grinned. "Ben is outspoken when it comes to my family. And protective as well. He and Molly are like the relatives we never had."

"Then that explains his concern."

Ty slid his fingers into the front pockets of his jeans. "Ben also has to realize I'm not a kid anymore. He can't get me out of trouble. And he has to stop interfering."

"That sounds like Molly's job."

He chuckled at that. "They've always been there for Ruby Sue. Can't complain about that."

Casey's brows drew together. "But they must be expressing the concern the other merchants feel. Everyone talks to Ben and Molly."

"Everyone just talks too much." He rested his hip against the sawhorse, his chest tightening when he thought about being the topic of conversation yet again.

Casey stepped toward him, concern etched on her face, compassion filling her eyes. God, she looked beautiful.

"Look, Ty. I admit, I don't know much of the current history around here, but I can read people. And the few folks I've spoken to are really worried about this. Why?"

He dug his hands deeper into his pockets. "I guess they're worried about who might be moving in."

"You must know, it's your firm."

"I'm not involved anymore." He didn't want to talk about the firm or Sabrina now. Ever. He wanted to close his eyes. Forget the past. Right now was all that mattered. Here, with Casey, the first woman he'd felt a flicker of interest in since his disaster of an engagement.

She moved inches closer just as a haunting love song came over the radio. Seconds passed as she gazed into his eyes, a slight look of confusion marring her brow. At that moment he couldn't help himself, it was as if he'd lost control of his senses. He reached out and brushed the back of his hand over the satiny skin of her cheek. Her eyes fluttered closed and she sighed, her breath fanning his fingers. He lowered his head, wanting nothing more than to brush his lips across hers.

In the distance, he heard a vague noise. He stubbornly pushed it from his consciousness, but the persistent ring made Ty realize the sound came from the telephone.

Casey jumped back, the wonder in her cloudy eyes turning to wariness. Ty took a deep breath, appalled at what he'd almost done, at how much of himself he'd given away.

Casey jogged into the kitchen and grabbed the phone. "Hello?"

"What's wrong with you? You sound out of breath."

"Bonnie? What is it? Anything wrong?"

"Just wanted to warn you. Before I locked up tonight Miles called. He doesn't have your new number."

Casey sank against the wall. Her voice went flat. "Did he say what he wanted?"

"He's looking for you. Says he wants to come see you and talk about . . . things."

A dark anger swept over Casey. "I told him I never wanted to see him again."

"Well, he's not listening. Maybe Miles wants you to come back to work." Her voice lowered as she failed to hide her concern. "You wouldn't go, would you? Even if you could make lots more money?"

"I don't care how much money he offers me." Casey looked across the room and saw Ty's eyes narrow at her words. She was too upset by this whole conversation to decipher his expression.

"Good. And I didn't give him your number."

"Thanks." Casey heard the phone click on the other end. She closed her eyes and took a cleansing breath. She hadn't spoken to Miles since coming to Paineville. Why on earth would he want to talk to her when he could be romancing his next sales executive? Something was up. She hoped it had nothing to do with Crafty Creations.

She placed the phone back in the cradle and peered into the living room. Heat rose on her face. She noticed the soft tingling on her lips, reminding her that she'd almost been kissed by Ty Banner.

Fearful of melting under his spell again, she stepped under the archway and glared at him. "So what was that all about? Trying to change the subject?"

His eyes grew dark. "It worked, didn't it?"

Biting the inside of her cheek, she mentally counted to ten. "Yes, it worked, but this conversation isn't over."

Ty bent down to retrieve his toolbox. "Yes. It is."

She blocked his path as he tried to pass her. "Wait. I want some answers here."

"I told you once that my life is off-limits. We have to spend time together while I finish working here, but that doesn't mean I'm going to bare my soul to you."

Casey backed away. He might be stubborn, but he had a point. She knew from day one that some corners of his heart were simply off-limits. She allowed him to win this round.

He halted and regarded her, forcing her to look straight into his eyes. He stood so near she could feel the heat emanating from his body. "Look. I was out of line earlier. It won't happen again."

"You're right about that. But you're not off the hook yet. I still intend to find out what's going on."

"So do I," he muttered and walked out the back door.

Ty caught up with Marilyn later that day at his grandmother's place. Ruby Sue was up to her elbows in flour as she alternately kneaded dough and formed pie crusts, all in honor of the Founder's Day celebration and a visit from their brother, Gabe. She shouted out instructions to Marilyn, who had forgone her usual suit and donned jeans and a T-shirt, already smeared with blueberry juice.

"Hey, Ruby Sue," he drawled as he kissed her flour-dappled cheek.

She nodded in reply. "Git over to that stool and stir up those peaches."

The house held the familiar smells Ty always loved—the sweet scent of fruit and yeasty dough. As he sauntered around the table, he deliberately planted a hearty kiss on Marilyn's cheek. She kept her eyes downcast and pursed her lips together.

"The silent treatment won't work with me," Ty said. "You've got some explaining to do."

Ruby Sue stopped her motions and leveled her eyes with his. "I won't stand for arguing in my kitchen."

"I don't plan on arguing. I just want some information that only my dear sister can give me." He indicated the back door with a nod of his head.

Marilyn reluctantly wiped off her hands. Ty grabbed

her elbow and propelled her outside. She shrugged
him off and walked to the far side of the porch, her
back rigid.

Ty broke the silence. "What's going on?"

"What do you mean?"

He sighed. So she wanted to play that game. "Why
is my firm coming up to work on the building space
in the square?"

"It's not just your firm," she reminded him. "I asked
John to come up and give me an estimate on what
work needed to be done. As usual the rumors are out
of control. John can't actually go in there until I get
the owner to sell."

Ty still didn't like the idea. He'd started the legal
proceedings to separate himself from John and the
business. But even still, he didn't like John slinking
around behind his back.

She didn't say anything more, so Ty walked up behind her, squinting into the midday sun as he looked
off into the woods. "You've been elusive lately, Marilyn. Under the circumstances, I guess John didn't have
to say a word about this job when I was in Atlanta.
Still, it makes me wonder what you two are up to."

As she twirled around, Ty noticed her face lined
with fatigue and sadness. "You just have to trust me.
I'm working on a deal that will be good for all of us."

"I trusted your opinion once and ended up with Sabrina." He frowned at his sister's stricken look. "I
don't like digging up ancient history, but if I remember correctly, you wanted me to move up in the world.
You thought money, and Sabrina, would make me

happy. And you thought you'd sail along on my coat-tails. Move up in the world and make a name for your-self. It didn't work, Sis. I thought you'd have seen that by now."

Tears glistened in her eyes. "Ty, there's just so much pressure at work. I can't explain, I just have to—"

"Marilyn, you've made a success of yourself. You've made piles of money. You dug yourself out of our sorry past. Don't you think it's time to slow down?"

She clamped her jaw tight.

"Look, all the money in the world doesn't change where we came from, so be proud of your accomplish-ments. There's nothing worse than having a bank full of money and a big empty house to share it with. Be careful, honey."

A mutinous look passed over her face. "Don't butt into my life, Ty."

"Then you stay out of mine. Don't make a deal with John." That said, he strode into the kitchen.

Ruby Sue glanced up at him as he walked in. "Got it all settled?"

"I doubt it." He snatched up a glass from the drainer and went to the refrigerator for some orange juice. A blast of cold air assaulted him when he opened the door, cooling his skin and his temper.

"Don't get her all upset. I need help with the pies and that girl has the touch."

She was right. As usual. And he hated it. "Sorry, Ruby Sue."

"Humph." The old woman kneaded dough until Ty

thought she'd hurt herself. He guessed that's what kept her going, hard work and concern about her family.

"When's Gabe coming in?" he asked, knowing the topic of his brother would get the subject off him.

"Should be tonight. They're driving up. Gabe wanted to spend some time with Emily."

Ty smiled. His ten-year-old niece had them all wrapped around her finger. Since the death of the girl's mother five years earlier, they'd all been making efforts to keep her happy. "Talked him into moving back yet?"

"No luck. The law firm keeps him too busy. He'll come when the time's right." She rolled out the flour mixture, then regarded him with a shrewd look. "Heard you've been keepin' busy at the old Winston place."

"Make that the Hudson place now."

Ruby Sue shrugged. "Can't. That'll always be old Thad Winston's place."

His grandmother was stubborn, as well as sly. He'd stayed away so he wouldn't have to have this conversation with her. He knew she couldn't leave it alone.

"So, tell me about her," she coaxed, while carefully scooping the fruit filling into the dough.

"She and her cousin own a shop on the town square, which means they're heavily into making money."

"Not everyone is Sabrina."

"Nothing like cutting to the punch."

Ruby Sue cackled. "I don't want to hear any excuses. Just give this Miss Hudson a try."

"This isn't something I can try on for size and return if it doesn't fit."

"Don't be obtuse, Tyrone."

Ruby Sue was the only person on earth who could call him by his given name and get away with it. And to really make her point, she always managed to use his name after reciting some big word she'd learned during her Building a Better Vocabulary phase. He loved this woman.

He placed the glass on the counter. "I don't plan on being around long enough to date anyone."

"You will. I saw the way your eyes lit up when I mentioned her name. You're more than ready to date again. Stop feelin' sorry for yourself. It's not becoming, Tyrone."

A shudder passed through him. He begrudgingly realized his grandmother was right. He liked Casey. He liked her spirit and determination, the way she'd come to care about this town. And he was growing more attracted to her as the days went by. Trouble was, he had no idea what to do about it.

Until he reconciled himself with the past, how could he start a future? He knew he shouldn't compare Casey with Sabrina, they were worlds apart. But the idea of becoming involved with a driven woman kept him gun-shy. And Casey definitely wanted her business to succeed. Didn't their argument prove it?

He really had to think about this.

"I'll consider your advice, but for now, I'm outta here. Let me know when Gabe shows up."

"I will. And you think about what I said. You need someone in your life, don't kid yourself that you don't."

"Yes, Ma'am." He saluted and escaped out the back door.

Chapter Five

Casey had forgotten how hot the summer months could get, even here in the mountains. And this weekend proved to be a scorcher. The sun hung bright and hot in the clear blue sky. Not so much as a simple breeze fluttered by to cool the air. The rich scent of hot earth collided with the savory aroma of barbeque. Hoots of laughter and squeals from excited children added to the festive atmosphere of Founder's Day.

Giving in to the heat, Casey wore a white tank top and denim shorts with flat, strappy, sandals, reminding herself fifty times that she wasn't there to impress anyone. Least of all Ty Banner.

But when she caught a glimpse of him across the town center, standing tall with the sunlight gleaming off his thick, dark hair, her stomach dipped in protest. Jet-black sunglasses obscured his eyes, matching his equally dark T-shirt. Even in this sultry air, he wore faded blue jeans and boots.

Would he notice her standing here? Oh brother! Who was she kidding? Of course she wanted to catch his eye. What woman wouldn't?

She watched as he concluded his conversation with a young man and turned his head in her direction. Lifting his glasses to rest on the crown of his head, he caught her stare, holding it with his. The temperature shot up ten more degrees, along with her heart rate. He didn't smile at first, just nodded his head in acknowledgment. Just when she thought he'd decided not to bother with her, he walked straight in her direction.

Panic set in as he weaved his way through the milling crowd, waving flags, and festive streamers fluttering all around him. His denim-clad legs moved quickly to close the space between them, his shoulders swaying with easy confidence. Casey swore she'd just been transported to heaven.

"Decided to brave the crowds?" he asked, coming to a halt before her. She looked up from his chest and saw the humor in his eyes.

"There's still a lot of folks I haven't met yet. I thought today would be a good chance to do that." Her breath caught in her throat when she noticed his scrutinizing gaze. Suddenly she felt fifteen again, gawky and unsure of herself. Casey tried to think of something witty and urbane to say, but all logical thought left her as she stared at Ty.

He pointed to the ground. "So what do you call that color?"

"Excuse me?"

"The polish on your toes. What's it called?"

"Passion Flower."

"Figures." He looked down, then back up at her with a wolfish grin. "I like it."

To take her mind off the liquid heat sizzling through her veins, Casey took a barrette from her pocket and lifted her hair onto her head, clipping it into place. With nervous jerks she tugged wisps around her ears, noticing that Ty hadn't taken his eyes from her the entire time. His intense study sent fleeting chills over her feverish skin.

The flu, she decided. She must be getting the flu.

"Uncle Ty." A high-pitched squeal came from behind Ty, ending Casey's sweet torment.

Ty turned toward the sound just in time to catch a young girl pitching herself at him with all her might. She giggled in delight, throwing her arms around Ty's neck in a tight grasp. He took a few teetering steps back before gaining his balance.

His voice was muffled against her cheek. "Hey, girl. I've been missing you."

She leaned back in his arms. "And I missed you, too. I'm glad Daddy decided to come home for a visit."

"You just keep reminding him that this is home," Ty teased as he set her on the ground.

Casey's chest squeezed tight when she viewed the loving expression on his face. The ever-present fatigue lines disappeared and his inner light shone through. In that moment, Casey knew she was lost to him.

"Who's that?" asked the girl. She took hold of her uncle's hand, swinging it back and forth.

"Miss Casey Hudson," Ty introduced. "And this is my niece, Emily."

The girl squinted at Casey. "Is she your girlfriend?"

Casey went still, waiting to hear Ty's reply.

"No, honey. Just a friend."

"That's too bad," Emily said, matter-of-factly. "Gran says you need a good woman to get you out of the house."

Casey inhaled a stunned breath and looked at Ty. To her astonishment, an endearing shade of red stained his cheeks.

Ty hugged his niece again before she ran off to another group of friends. "Ruby Sue says way too much, especially in front of kids."

"No problem," Casey said, amazed at Ty's reaction to his niece's announcement.

They stood in silence before Casey noticed a steady shift in the crowd. Families headed toward the curbs along the edges of the green, finding a place to settle down and watch the parade. She wondered what it would be like one day with a family of her own. Shaking her head, she glanced at her watch. "Five minutes till show time."

"Did you bring a lawn chair or blanket to sit on?"

She frowned. "No, I didn't even think of it."

Ty grinned. "It's a good thing we met up. I have a blanket spread out under a shady tree on the other side of the park. Away from my family." He held out his hand. "C'mon."

How could she resist? She nodded, but instead of

taking her hand, he placed his palm on the small of her back. The possessive pressure seared through her clothes as they twisted through the crowd to reach Ty's special spot. A dozen other people had the same idea of escaping under the shade, making the space on the blanket much smaller than she'd anticipated.

As they sat, the shrill siren of a fire engine sounded in the distance, signaling the start of the procession. The sound faded, followed by the steady beat of bass drums and brass instruments. The sweet scent of cotton candy wafted by as a vendor called out for any takers. A family of young children squealed with delight as their father bought each one a wand of the airy confection. Other peddlers displayed patriotic-colored pinwheels, baseball pendants, and helium balloons.

Casey smiled with delight. Her parents never liked attending the town parades, deciding instead to travel to Atlanta and the big-city attractions or stay ensconced at home, away from the cheering crowds. Because they wouldn't let her go, she'd sneaked out a few times with Bonnie, but never enough to suit her. She loved these events.

"It's been years since I've done anything like this. I'd forgotten how much small-town traditions still hold true."

Ty reached behind her and rested his hand on the blanket to anchor his weight. He leaned so close, their shoulders brushed. "It's easy to run away from tradition, but harder to feel a part of it again."

She opened her mouth to agree as the crowd started clapping. Casey turned her attention from Ty's comment to the main street, just in time to see a bright, silver, convertible Cadillac come into view.

Red, white, and blue streamers adorned the hood. Balloons hovered overhead, attached to the side-view mirrors. Behind the wheel sat a portly man dressed as an original founder, puffing on a huge cigar. He waved to the crowd, laughing, yelling, and carrying on.

The Caddy passed by, followed by the high school marching band. The volume of the music didn't lend itself to conversation, so Casey settled back to enjoy the rendition of a patriotic Broadway song.

Ty moved closer, the length of his arm braced intimately along her back. She felt the power radiating from him, the sheer maleness of him. It felt natural, normal, like he belonged by her side. Those thoughts had been recurring lately, ever since she'd first spoken to him after fifteen years. Their lives might have gone in different directions, but they were thrown together now. And because of that, she planned to see where this 'thing' between them was headed.

It might not be the smartest move of her life, she thought, but she couldn't deny the tingling of excitement in her stomach every time she was in close proximity to Ty.

"Oh, look." Casey pointed as a battalion of children on bicycles rode by in formation, a rainbow of multi-colored streamers weaving through the spokes, whirling round and round as they cycled by. She leaned over and spoke in Ty's ear. "That's Bonnie's son leading the pack."

The final group, dressed in period costume representing the original town founders, marched with pride and dignity. They received salutes and claps of appreciation.

All too soon, the tail end of the parade arrived. The crowd drifted into the street and down the road to the town park, where the food and games were located. Since Ty made no move to follow, Casey was content to stay with him and people-watch. Only a few stragglers remained before he spoke.

"When I was a kid, I always watched the parade from a tree down the block."

Casey pulled her knees up in front of her, wrapping her arms around them. "Why was that?"

Ty stared at the departing crowd, a faraway look in his eyes. "We never were welcome much here. Most women didn't want my mother around, and she knew it, so we usually stayed home. Until I got old enough to be curious. By then, I didn't care what my mother wanted. I did my own thing." A tight smile stretched across his lips. "Even if it meant climbing a tree to keep out of sight."

Casey hugged her knees close. "My folks thought this whole picnic idea was hokey. They couldn't wait to leave."

She felt Ty shift his weight, but he didn't leave her side. "Guess our folks had the same way of thinking. Except one thought they were too good and the other thought they weren't good enough. Bottom line, neither wanted anything to do with this town."

The sense of camaraderie at the moment let her ask questions she normally wouldn't have dared before today. "Where's your Mom now?"

She felt his muscles tense. "I'm not sure," he said

in a strained voice. "Last we heard she'd married some guy in Houston."

Silence settled between them before Casey spoke again. "At least you had your grandmother to raise you. From what I've heard, everyone loves her."

"That wasn't always so. My mother managed to ruin any decent reputation our family had. And with my father running off, well, Ruby Sue had a lot of messes to clean up."

"She survived. All of you did."

A humorless curve pulled his lips. "Yeah, but it wasn't easy." He turned his attention to her. "How about you?"

She shrugged. "My parents didn't worry about what I did."

"Ruby Sue worried enough for all of us." This time Ty's smile was sincere. "She's the only person I've ever been afraid of. The thought of her whupping my bottom was scarier than any horror movie we would sneak into at the old drive-in."

He plucked a piece of grass and twisted it between his fingers. "She kept me on the straight and narrow and I appreciate that."

"We all need someone like that in our lives."

"Did you have anyone like that after you left town?" he asked.

Casey tilted her head. Her hair fell over her cheek and she brushed it away. "No. I relied on myself. My parents were always busy, so I decided what career I wanted, then went after it. Eventually it led me back here." She grinned. "Guess I was meant to be a small-town girl."

"Well, small-town girl, we have a picnic to attend." Ty jumped up and held out his hand. "Come on, let's see if Ruby Sue won the ribbon for her pies."

Casey clasped his outstretched hand, loving his strength as he yanked her to her feet. He didn't release his grip, but tugged her to him, slowly and with purpose. His eyes focused on her lips. She held her breath, waiting for his next move. An unexpected breeze lifted the tendrils of hair around her face and cooled her flushed skin.

Ty gently touched her neck with his roughened fingers. Casey felt the tingling sensation all the way to her toes. How she wished he would kiss her.

"Hey, Bro. Don't you know there's a statute against outright displays of affection in a public place?"

Casey flinched and Ty immediately dropped his hand, as if touching her a moment longer would do him bodily harm. A flash of guilt crossed his face as he bent down to retrieve the blanket.

"Don't you know it's impolite to interrupt a couple of friends who are getting reacquainted?" Ty countered.

"We haven't been introduced. I'm Gabe Banner."

Casey returned his handshake as she viewed the attractive man before her. He was just as tall as Ty, and built just as broadly, but his hair was lighter, his eyes a steel gray. Even though he smiled, a sadness lingered in the depths. Faint lines bracketed his mouth. Despite that, Casey immediately felt comfortable with him. "Nice to meet you."

He grinned. "Yeah, but I bet you wish I had waited a while longer before cutting in."

As Gabe gave Ty a healthy bear hug, Casey felt her cheeks heat up. How right he was. Maybe he'd arrived at the right time, before she and Ty made their attraction public. The idea of them becoming grist for the rumor mill made her grateful that Gabe had showed up.

"Why don't we join the others," Gabe suggested, after the prolonged silence. "Gran's pies should be being judged right about now."

He started off before them. Ty hung back, a sheepish grin curving his features. Casey's heart leapt.

"Sorry about that. Guess I lost my head."

Casey waved her hand. "Me too. We should be careful about that in the future."

Ty's smile faded. Falling into step behind Gabe, Ty made sure he kept close to her. Her heart leapt. She could get used to this.

They entered the throng just as the emcee, resplendent in the replica clothing of a miner, spoke into the microphone. The town had built up around the discovery of a gold vein that ran through the north central mountains of Georgia. Local history remained a strong part of the heritage the townspeople shared. Growing up here, it bound Casey to one big family.

Ty took Casey's hand, leading her through the crowd to the place where his family loyally surrounded their grandmother. She savored the warmth of his firm grasp, this step toward . . . what, she wasn't sure. As the family parted to let them in, Casey got a glimpse of the matriarch.

Casey felt a jolt of surprise as she viewed the woman. Even though Ruby Sue sat on a lawn chair,

Casey could tell she was of small stature, finely boned and petite, but nevertheless, regal. She held Emily on her lap and spoke into her granddaughter's ear. Emily laughed and pointed, but Ruby Sue grabbed her hand and brought it to the girl's lap. Emily just laughed louder.

As if sensing their presence, Ruby Sue turned and looked Casey squarely in the eye. In those eyes Casey read determination and a strength that belied her size. From that look alone, Casey understood where Ty got his strength of will.

She also sensed it would take a great deal of patience to work her way into Ty's heart. More important, she wondered if Ty would fight her if she tried and if she'd be left to tumble head-long into heartache.

Ty moved from her side to embrace his grandmother. The love between them flowed strongly. And Casey knew it came from a determined woman, guiding her charges when they were young.

As she watched Ty, Casey realized he was completely different from most of the men she knew. She liked and respected him. Did he feel the same about her?

A loud shout brought Casey's thoughts to the present. She focused on Ruby Sue. The older woman's eyes narrowed, as if she'd read Casey's mind. A chill ran down her spine. Did the old woman know something she didn't?

A rousing cheer went up as Ruby Sue's name came across the speakers. The emcee winked in her direction, making a big show of tasting the pie. Casey guessed that it was a forgone conclusion. Ruby Sue was the town favorite and most likely the grand prize winner.

Before long, the taste test concluded and the judges huddled to make the final decision. Casey listened in on the family bantering, suddenly feeling a bit lonely and out of place. Her parents never would have joined this merry crowd. She'd missed so much because of that. Still, Casey longed for a family that enjoyed the small pleasures of life. Like Ty and his family obviously did.

"You okay?" Ty whispered in her ear.

She jumped, annoyed he had caught her musing. Once again she wondered when he had grown so aware of her mood changes. Her retort sounded sharp. "I'm fine."

He frowned, dark brows angling over hooded eyes. Before he could speak again, the emcee bellowed into the microphone. "And the winner of this year's pie contest is none other than Ruby Sue Callahan."

The crowd responded with wild clapping and whistles. Emily twisted on her grandmother's lap to hug her tightly. Pride blazed in all three Banner siblings. The love for their grandmother and the closeness of the family made her acutely aware that she was an outsider.

Suddenly gripped with emotions that she didn't want to define, Casey slipped away from Ty and headed back toward the square. She had to get away from the close-knit family. They reflected her hidden dream, the one she'd tucked into the back of her heart, taken out during those lonely times when she wished for a loving family. Wished for parents who stayed at home to be with their only child. Wished she could have family to hug and hold. Unlike her own.

Before she could escape to sort out her thoughts, Bonnie called her name. She stopped, searching for her cousin.

"Casey," she said, walking swiftly toward her. "Come here. There's someone you have to meet."

Casey tamped down the personal ache within her and joined her cousin. Bonnie pointed to a tall man with burnished blond hair, his broad back to them, conversing with Bonnie's husband, Chuck. The man turned, a smile lighting his tanned face. She didn't recognize him immediately, then memory kicked in. Ty's old partner in crime.

Casey smiled. "Mike Post, our resident artist. Your work is incredible."

Mike shook her hand, his artist's grip strong and sure. "Well, not a permanent resident, but close enough." He stepped back and regarded Casey. "And you're the marketing genius who is going to sell my work so I don't have to travel so much."

Casey enjoyed his praise. "That's the plan."

His expression grew serious. "When Bonnie explained what you had in mind, I jumped at the idea. I'm at a point in my career where I want to travel less. I have a new studio in Asheville and I want to concentrate on new projects. You'll allow me to do that."

"I'm so glad. The website is almost ready to feature your work. I've been meaning to get in touch to find out if you have a site of your own. If you do, we can link and reach more people," Casey replied.

"I don't have much time for computers, but a friend

has agreed to set up a website for me. I'll give you the information you need to contact him."

"You are planning to come to the store and see your display, aren't you?" Casey asked.

"That's one of the reasons I'm here."

Bonnie, uncharacteristically quiet throughout the conversation, piped in. "And the other reason?"

Casey elbowed her cousin. "Bonnie. Maybe Mike would rather not—"

"It's okay," Mike cut in. He chuckled. "I'm used to Bonnie's questions. She's already quizzed me on my personal life. And no, I'm not married, but that's another reason I'm settling down. Someone back home has my full and total interest."

"So, besides the store," Bonnie prompted, "your reason for being here is . . . ?"

Mike's smile faded. "Walking up right now."

Casey looked over her shoulder to see Ty purposely striding toward them. His face was blank; once again she couldn't read the emotion there. But his hands were fisted, his long legs easily crossing the ground between them. She could read the tension that radiated from him. Finally he stood before them, glancing first at Casey, then at Mike.

"Long time," Ty said, his tone flat.

"I intend to rectify that," Mike replied.

Chapter Six

T y managed to control the unwarranted surprise and underlying regret at seeing Mike after all these years. He hadn't known what to expect when he saw the man he had once considered his best friend. Raw emotions about the past washed over him.

He noticed Mike's eyes widen when he approached, then return to normal calm. He hoped his face mirrored Mike's.

He held out his hand. "Good to see you." *Weak, but honest and to the point.*

Mike nodded and clasped his hand in a firm shake. "Same here."

Ty's gaze roamed over the group standing around him. He didn't stop long enough to gauge Casey's reaction. His eyes returned to his old friend's and he saw a warming there. Taking that to heart, he hoped Casey's suggestion that Mike wanted to resume their friendship had credence. He also knew it was his responsibility to take the first step.

"In town for long?" he asked.

"A few days."

"Mike is going to check out Crafty Creations before he leaves." Casey's smile brightened her entire face. She glowed when she talked about her business.

Ty felt jealousy toward her store rearing its ugly head again. Every time she mentioned the store he felt a gap widen between them. Which didn't make a whole lot of sense. They had agreed to a certain attraction between them, but didn't it stop there?

If he did take things with Casey to the next level, then maybe he'd have room to complain. But the idea of a serious relationship still gave him pause, even with someone like Casey. She had everything a guy could want: good looks and an independent streak that he could admire.

But her tenacious desire to make it on her own sent off warning bells. She made it clear that she didn't need a guy to get where she wanted to go. She took pride in getting there by herself.

He kept reminding himself over and over that she was just a friend, someone he used to know, not the be-all and end-all to his existence. She was a person with her own life. Just like him. If her work bothered him, then that was his problem, not hers.

"How about checking out the store now?" Mike suggested, checking his wristwatch. "It's going to take the coordinators a while to get organized for the games. We have at least a half hour. I want to see what you've done to display my carvings."

"Want to join us?" Casey asked Ty, placing her hand on his arm. For encouragement with Mike? he wondered. He'd shared about his past and he knew she'd try to get them to reconcile.

But he wouldn't be a third wheel if Mike didn't want him around. Until this minute, he hadn't realized just how much he'd missed that friendship. And how much he wanted it back.

Chalk another one up for Casey. She must have sensed how much he wanted to clear things up with Mike. And leave it to her to make things right. That was just one more precious thing about her he admired.

She tilted her head when he didn't reply, her forehead wrinkled. "I'm sure Mike would love to show off his work."

Mike stared straight at Ty. "C'mon with us."

Not wanting to appear overly curious, Ty nodded. Besides, he'd never been to the store. He supposed now was as good time as any.

He followed the small group back to the square, with Bonnie chattering the entire way. Mike laughed at her stories, transporting Ty back to the carefree time of their youth, when they were poised on the brink of successful futures, ready to tackle the world and make it their own.

Casey unlocked the door and hurried inside to turn off the alarm while Ty trailed behind the others. A homey scent permeated the store, reminding him of something he tried to recall, something from his childhood, but it eluded him. Maybe it reminded him of Ruby Sue's pies. Either way, a sense of well-being streamed over him, surprising him, since he'd had mixed feelings about entering the place that Casey's life revolved around.

Gazing around, he took inventory of her business. The merchandise was set up to the customer's advantage, all laid out within hand's reach. She'd obviously spent long hours arranging the shelves and display cases in a way that would draw interest. A grudging pride welled up within him. She was good at her job. Had he ever really doubted it?

Yeah, she'd be successful, but would money spoil the person she was? For her sake, he hoped not. There were too many Sabrinas in the world, and not enough women like Casey. Every day proved more and more just how special she was. And how much he was really starting to care for her.

As if feeling her eyes on him, Ty met her expectant gaze. If he didn't know better, he'd swear she was holding her breath, waiting for his reaction. He grinned and she rewarded him with a jubilant smile.

"Would you like a tour?" she asked.

"Sure. Give me the works."

She took his hand, beaming with pride, and guided him around the store, telling him about the different artists' works. Bonnie and her husband lingered with Mike up front to get his input on the display.

When they reached the rear of the store, Ty tugged Casey's hand, dragging her into the back room.

"What are you doing?" she asked, her voice full of laughter.

"I want to see everything."

She laughed out loud, clapping her hand over her

mouth to muffle the sound and not arouse the curiosity of the others. "Do you like what you've seen so far?" she asked, questions reflected in her eyes.

"I'm impressed," he told her. "This is a first-class operation. And so are you."

"You think so?" She regarded him with hooded eyes. "Don't tell me you're one of those men who doesn't think a woman could make go of it in business."

"No way. Look at my sister, she's done okay for herself in the business world."

"Then I guess I shouldn't doubt the compliment."

"I heard a 'but' in that."

"But . . . you seem to be surprised by my success."

He glanced around the storeroom. "I've only seen you at home." He frowned, trying to put his thoughts into words. "Your focus is so deliberate. You spend hours on the computer, then hours here. Now I'm standing in the fruit of your labor. I guess I didn't put you and the reality of the store together." His lips turned up in a grin. "It's really top-notch."

Casey lowered her lashes and stared at his chest. She spoke in a hushed voice. "That means a lot to me. The people most important in my life don't seem to think I have what it takes." She looked up at him. "My father thinks I have to hold on to a man for dear life in order to be a success."

"You've proved him wrong."

She smiled again, gratitude shining in her chocolate-colored eyes. "I don't ever plan to rely on anyone for my livelihood again," she said with a firmness of conviction.

A coldness settled over him. His first instinct had been right, this woman would be trouble. He recognized the early warning signs. This was just the beginning, he knew. Step one. Like Sabrina, she made her future plans clear. No one would get in her way. Even if he got involved, her business would still come first. And he'd vowed never to be second best to a woman's relentless ambition again.

He dropped his hands and stepped away, maintaining control so as not to bolt from the room.

"What is it?" she asked in confusion.

"I just keep forgetting that we agreed not to get involved in each other's lives. Just business between us, remember? This store reminded me of that."

She shoved her hands onto her hips. "What does having my own business have to do with us?" Her voice rose. "I mean, if there is an *us*."

He didn't like the implication, but had to be honest with her. "We almost kissed each other in front of half the population in Paineville. That would definitely constitute our relationship as an *us*."

"Listen here," she poked him in the chest, her indignation making her even more appealing. "Just because you have a painful past doesn't mean you can take it out on me. You turn your emotions on and off so much I don't know what to think. But get this, I am successful and I'll remain successful, regardless of our relationship."

His eyes narrowed. Step two. She was fervently affirming her vow to put business number one. "I've heard that before."

Anger flashed across her flushed face. "From your

ex-fiancée, I suppose? Don't you *ever* compare me
with her. I don't know all the details, but from what
I've hear, she was a user. And if you're comparing
her to me . . . then I'm sorry you feel that way."

Casey pursed her lips together, then opened her
mouth as if to say more, but slammed it shut. She
jerked away, but not before Ty glimpsed the threat of
tears caused by his rejection, the sheen of moisture
she refused to blink away. She heaved a heavy breath,
then stormed out of the back room.

Ty ran a hand over his eyes. Why hadn't he just
kept his mouth shut? Was he so stubborn in his resolve
not to get involved with Casey that he had to pick a
fight?

He started after her, but Mike Post appeared at the
doorway, blocking his escape. "Woman trouble?" his
deep, amused voice asked. Ty backed off as Mike
lounged against the door frame.

"Is there any other kind?" he grumbled.

"I see some things haven't changed."

Ty stepped over to a worktable, composing his jum-
bled thoughts about Casey before talking to Mike. He
rested against the solid furniture and crossed his arms
over his chest. "Never could get it right."

"You did before Sabrina came along."

"I did a lot of things before Sabrina came along."

"You know where I stood on that relationship. I
thought it was doomed from the start. For a pretty
smart guy, you fell for her like a ton of bricks."

"Thanks for the compliment," Ty said, with a humorless laugh.

Mike pushed his hands into the pockets of his

shorts. "Hey, I'm only speaking the truth. And from what I've heard, you seem to be hiding from it."

Ty couldn't help himself; he allowed himself to ask, "Hiding from what truth?"

"Do you really want to hear it?"

Ty crossed his feet at the ankles. "I asked, didn't I?"

"Okay." Mike crossed the room to look out the back grated window, then turned to face Ty full-on. "Number one. You knew Sabrina was a gold digger. I told you that from the start. But you thought she'd be different with you. I'm afraid you learned that lesson the hard way."

Ty started to protest, but Mike held up a hand to halt his words. "I have the floor here, let me finish. Sabrina used you, but look on the flip side to see what she did for you. With both of your egos and ambitions, she urged you to start your own business. If I remember correctly, you were unsure about that."

Ty nodded but remained silent.

"So, once you got the local business going, she wanted Atlanta. And you went for it. Did it help your reputation? Yes. In fact, you could have plenty of work if you wanted."

Mike paused to admire another artist's work, probably to give Ty time to digest his words.

"Number two. From what I've heard since I've been back, you need to get off your duff and start living in the present. I know Sabrina hurt you. I know you're still bitter. But life goes on, buddy, with or with her."

Mike was right. Ty knew it deep in his gut. His heart just wasn't getting the connection and he wasn't ready to deal with the bitterness inside him. "Thanks for the advice, but I'd rather not to talk about Sabrina."

Mike shrugged. "Whatever. But I remember the old Ty. You were pretty confident in high school. Even had a thing for Casey back then."

"Yeah. Then she left."

"Not everyone leaves, you know."

Ty stared down at his boots, then back at his friend. "Guess I'm the one who left this friendship."

"I understood."

"Still doesn't make it right."

A shadow passed over Mike's face. "When I consider Sabrina as the source, it's easy to make allowances. One of the reasons I agreed to let Casey and Bonnie show my work is because I wanted a connection with this community again. I wanted to see how my old friend was getting on with his life." He paused. "It doesn't look like he's doing so hot."

Ty pushed away from the table. "Look, I appreciate everyone's concern, but this is my life and I can take care of myself."

Mike frowned. "Hey, no skin off my nose. You want to brood and be lonely, have at it. I just want you to know I'm around if you need someone to go have a beer with."

"I appreciate it," Ty grudgingly answered. "We'd better get back to the picnic."

Mike started to speak again, but instead held out his hand.

Ty grasped it, his first real connection with an old friend he'd really missed. For long seconds they held on, the bond reestablished. Then Mike dropped his hand and led the way back to the store entrance.

Bonnie watched them approach with a telltale smile on her lips. Ty figured the news of his renewed friendship with Mike would be all over town before sundown. "Finished, boys?"

"Yeah. Let us out of here," Ty grumbled.

As she locked the door behind them, Mike said to Ty in a low tone, "Another word of advice, old buddy."

Ty frowned. "Is it necessary?"

"Yeah. Lighten up on Casey. If you'd just get over yourself, you'd find out what a prize she is."

Ty ground his teeth and left in search of his family. He'd take his niece for a long walk so he didn't have to listen to anyone. He'd had enough to last him until next spring. Enough talking, enough advice, enough of small-town gossip.

As he came up to the crowd, he heard shouts near the creek. A long, flat, grassy stretch of land ran along the water, the best place to have races. Ty headed toward his brother, whose head was visible above the people.

"Hey, Gabe. What's going on?"

Gabe slapped his brother on the back. "You made it. It's time for the three-legged race. We need you."

"I'm not much in the mood for games."

His brother grinned. "A loaded statement there, but I don't have time to debate it. Hurry, I found you a partner. She's shorter than you, but you'll manage."

Grabbed by the arm, Ty had no choice but to be dragged along by his brother. His niece must have conned Gabe into letting her race with him.

Gabe stooped down while Ty looked over his shoulder for Emily. Instead, he glimpsed Casey standing beside Gabe, her glare shooting daggers at him. Her arms were crossed stubbornly across her chest. Caught up in gawking at her, it was too late before he realized that the rope being tied to his ankle was joining him to Casey.

"I don't like this any better than you," she started without preamble. "But your brother tricked me. He told me I'd be partners with a sweet family member. I assumed it would be Emily."

"I never said it was Emily," Gabe said innocently from the ground below, still tangling with the rope.

Ty tried to frown, but found it impossible. Maybe he had a chance to make things right with Casey. "He got me, too," he replied, then said to his brother, "You always could sweet-talk the women."

Gabe grunted and yanked the rope, causing Casey to lose her balance and crash into Ty's chest. Her eyes flared with anger and Ty felt the heat down to the soles of his boots. He grabbed her by the waist, steadying her before they both tumbled over. "Whoa."

"Tell your brother to be more careful," she fumed, dragging herself out of his embrace, obviously unsettled by the whole situation.

"Hear that, Bro?"

"One more round and I'm finished." Gabe circled their calves once more and tied off the rope. He stood, wiping his hands. "Now, go whup 'em all!" he said, slapping Ty on the back and jumping out of their way.

Casey stood at Ty's side, her protests useless. No

matter how much she tried to pull away, some body part still touched him.

Ty laughed at her futile efforts. "I'm afraid we're going to have to put up with these close quarters till the race is over."

"Fine. Just don't enjoy this too much."

He laughed again, slipping his arm around her to support them. "Much as I know you won't like this, I suggest you put your arm around my waist for balance."

She scowled up at him but followed his instruction. "Now, let's work on walking together before the start."

Moving in unison, it took only minutes for them to become one. Ty had to admit she was a trooper. Given his earlier behavior, being roped to him was most likely not the highlight of her day.

They got in line with ten other couples. Gabe began mock-betting, and shouts of good luck came from Mike on the sidelines. Ty tightened his grip around Casey's waist and concentrated on the finish line ahead. A loud voice called from a megaphone: "One, two, three, go!"

Ty grabbed Casey close and took off. She stumbled, then clutched a bunch of shirt at his back and held on. With Casey valiantly keeping pace, he managed to lead them in front while other couples around them tripped or took a spill.

With his tugging, her shirt came loose from her shorts. Ty tried to grab hold of the hem, but his fingers slipped from the material. He paused for a second, giving them enough time to be thrown off balance.

Before he could right them, they careened toward the embankment of the creek alongside the grassy straight-away.

Ty tried to set them back on course, but Casey lost her hold on his shirt and floundered. "Tyrone Banner, what are you doing?" she cried as the water loomed closer.

Just at the bank, Ty jerked her to a stop. He caught his breath, steadying them. He wavered at the edge of the creek's shallow water. Ready to continue on, he yanked Casey flush up against him. She looked up into his eyes, her hair loose around her face, her cheeks flushed, and his heart went haywire.

She reached around him, circling both arms around his waist to keep her balance. That was his undoing. He leaned into her, ready to kiss her like he'd wanted to since she stormed out of the store. And she lifted her chin, her lips so close he could almost taste their sweetness.

She swayed into him. His boots lost their footing on the soggy mud. Casey's eyes widened and her hands gripped him harder.

They pitched headlong into the chilly stream.

Hoots of laughter greeted him as he struggled to keep Casey from hitting the creekbed and the scattered rocks. It didn't work. She landed as fully immersed in the water as he did. She came up splashing and sputtering, clamoring for air, groping at his shirt to keep herself upright. "What happened to you?" she asked between soggy gasps of air.

He brushed her wet hair from her face. "*You* happened to me," he said, gently brushing his finger over her lips.

She batted his dripping hand away. "Don't do this Ty. I can't keep up with this hot-and-cold game."

Properly chastised, Ty helped her out of the water. When they made it back onto the grass, he untied the ropes and threw them off to the side.

Casey stamped her cute feet. "Look at me," she moaned. "I'm drenched."

He took off his shirt and handed it to her. "Here. It's not much, but it'll cover you up some."

"Gee, thanks. A lot of good this will do." She rolled her eyes but grabbed the soaked garment, holding it in front of her tank top.

"It's all I've got."

"If it weren't for you, I wouldn't be soaked."

"Think of it as all in a day's work."

She humphed before marching off toward her cousin, who held out a blanket to wrap her in. Bonnie chattered nonstop, but Ty couldn't hear Casey's reaction.

She had every right to be exasperated with him. Just a short time ago he had rejected her in the store, and now here he was, dragging her into the cold water.

Casey pivoted on her heel and came back to him, holding out his shirt. It hadn't been much of an offer, but he didn't want Casey to be embarrassed in her soaked shirt. He also didn't want any of the men staring at her. He reserved that privilege all to himself.

She sighed and her expression softened from totally exasperated to slightly miffed. "Thanks," she said, holding out his shirt.

"It was the least I could do."

The emcee called for the next game to start. "It's hot today, your clothes will dry in no time," he offered.

A reluctant grin pulled at her lips. "So? Did we win?"

He returned the smile. "Nope."

"Oh well, I was never very good at competition." She started to walk away.

"Casey. Wait." She stopped as he approached her. "I'm sorry. For the things I said earlier. You're right, I can't keep treating you this way."

"I haven't done anything to you, Ty."

Yes you have, he silently admitted to himself. *You moved away all those years ago after high school, just when I wanted to know you better. Just when I was getting to know me better. And now you're back, making me feel things I buried long ago.*

"I know it's my problem and I'm not handling it right."

"Too bad for both of us." She spoke softly, compassion in her eyes. Then she gently brushed past him, her fragrance leaving a sultry trail behind her.

As Ty watched her leave, Gabe came up behind him. "Guess that wasn't such a good idea. By the way you two were looking at each other earlier, I thought maybe. . . ."

Ty sighed. "Probably not."

"Too bad. She seems like a great lady."

"That's the problem. I can't hurt her, Gabe."

"Then stop hurting yourself and let go of the past."

Ty turned his head. "Have you?"

Gabe blinked, his face a mask. "We're talking about you."

"I think you proved my point." Ty dropped his arm over his brother's shoulders. "We're pitiful, you know that?"

"Yeah, but you have a second chance here. Try not to blow it. If the roles were reversed, I'd hope you'd have the guts to tell me to stop being a jerk and go after a good thing when I see it."

"Be careful, little brother. It just may happen." He smiled at Gabe. "And thanks."

Gabe nodded and sauntered away, stopping to swing Emily up into his arms. Emily squealed in delight, then hugged her father.

Ty's chest tightened at the scene. He loved his family, he knew that much. So why did he have such a hard time allowing himself to fall for Casey?

Shaking his head, he wrung out his damp shirt and tossed it over his shoulders. What-if games had lost their appeal for him a long time ago.

Chapter Seven

"He's been looking for you," Bonnie announced as she led Casey to a quiet spot so she could dry off.

"Ty?" Casey asked, pushing down the telltale leap of excitement in her chest. She scanned the crowd, searching for his tall build, his steady stride. Despite the way he infuriated her, she couldn't help but search him out.

"No, not Ty. Miles. He called the store again."

Casey's short-lived elation came to an abrupt end. "When?"

"Yesterday, just after you left. I should have told you, but Chuck and the kids picked me up and we drove out to the Burger Palace. By the time we got home, I forgot."

"You could have mentioned this earlier today."

"I could have, but you were having such a good time with Ty. I didn't want to ruin your day."

Looking down at her wet clothes, then back at her cousin, Casey laughed. "So you wait till now to tell me? Thanks for the picker-upper."

"Hey, at least I told you," Bonnie reasoned.

Casey grimaced. One more thing to spoil her first Founder's Day in fifteen years. First, a harassing encounter with Ty. Now the news about Miles.

"You're gonna have to talk to him eventually," Bonnie said, squinting her eyes in the afternoon sun.

"I know," Casey sighed, using the blanket to dry the dripping ends of her hair. "I've been putting it off."

"Dread seeing him?"

She nodded. "Only because I know he wants me to come back to work. There's no way I'm moving back to Cincinnati."

"Then you don't miss him? Romantically?" Bonnie pried.

"How could you even ask that?"

"Just wanted to be sure." Bonnie grinned. "I know you have a thing for Ty. And with you getting all upset about that dip in the creek, I didn't want you going off and doing something stupid."

"I've done a few stupid things in my life, but going back to Miles will *not* be one of them."

Bonnie let out a relieved breath. "Good."

Of course, hoping for a future with Ty wasn't too smart, especially in his current frame of mind. If only that tug of attraction wasn't so strong. If only she didn't want more than he could offer.

He'd made his intentions quite clear. Business only. And she'd comply, no matter how much her insides ached. After all, she had her own independence to think about.

But Bonnie was right about one thing.

Casey definitely had a thing for Ty.

Sidetracked by her impromptu dip in the creek, Casey decided to forgo the remainder of the team games. Her clothes finally dried so it was safe to abandon the blanket. Instead of roaming around, she remained close to Bonnie and her family, careful to stay out of Ty's path.

"Men."

"What was that?" Bonnie looked at her and laughed.

"I'm so glad I only dated Miles, never getting really romantically involved. We tried it . . . but it never felt right."

"It wasn't the real thing. Trust me, you know the genuine article when it comes along."

"Like you and Chuck?"

"Yep. Fell for him at first sight."

"You guys have a wonderful relationship." Casey breathed deeply, the pain of the past still cutting through her. "In one swoop, Miles took my job and my happiness away from me. I worked hard to cultivate leads and woo perspective clients."

"I bet that's why he wants you back."

"He may think I'll fail, but he's wrong. Even if he came crawling on his knees, I wouldn't leave Paineville."

"Good for you."

That's right. I don't need anyone's approval. The numbers speak for themselves. The store is doing great, and I intend to keep it that way."

Bonnie gave her a thumbs-up. "I have no doubt that you will."

Near dusk, the men started work on the great bonfire while the women readied the marshmallows and children ran off to gather strong sticks for roasting. An impromptu song broke out as everyone bided time until the real show began.

At nine o'clock precisely, the final event of the night would kick off: fireworks. Loud, brilliant, spectacular explosions in the sky. Children would ooh and aah as they watched the black sky explode into a kaleidoscope of light.

Casey sat by herself, mulling over the upcoming fireworks and the lack of sparkle in her love life. That is, until Ty came back into the picture. He'd managed to set her in a tailspin when she thought she had everything figured out. As the darkness gathered around her, she realized that Ty's role in her life was not clear, just like the shifting shadows surrounding her. And she liked things brightly lit and on a firm path.

As families gathered by the fire, Casey grew antsy. She needed to work off this restless energy that thoughts of Ty stirred up in her.

Taking a chance that she might run into him, she meandered through the park. He was nowhere in sight, so she people-watched, catching glimpses of husbands and wives and their children. Some faces she remembered from her years in high school here. They had opted to stay in town, maintaining family ties and keeping treasured traditions. Were they really better off in the long run?

The tightening of her heart was at odds with her

firm resolve to be successful in business. She couldn't have both, could she? So far, that hadn't worked for her, and with the way things were going with Ty, she didn't see any change in the near future.

She waved to one couple, thinking back to simpler times, teenage years when a crush was all-consuming and all-important. Her memory went back to her short time with Ty that long ago summer.

He had never confided in her about his family problems, but even back then she sensed a deep hurt in him. He joked about living in a trailer and not having money or a mother, but the humor was laced with bitterness. Being young and not very worldly, she couldn't offer advice. She just listened, like a friend would do. Only she had started to think of him as more than just a friend and, at her young age, it frightened her.

He had a tough guy reputation. Although he was popular, especially with the girls, there seemed to be a boundary that some wouldn't let him cross. And he knew that. It made his outer armor all the more tough.

She'd desperately hoped he'd see her as old enough to take to a party, not as a young and naive fifteen-year-old. Nevertheless, a bond had formed. She didn't ask for more than that.

A honking horn jostled Casey out of her memories. To her surprise, she found herself behind the General Store. Here, the culmination of all her youthful memories came together. She'd shared her first kiss with Ty here. How could she ever forget that night?

"Guess you couldn't forget this place either."

She started, immediately recognizing the deep voice that came from out of the twilight.

She turned and saw Ty, her past and present colliding the moment he spoke. He was leaning against the building. "I . . . I was just leaving," she said, unsure if she could trust herself to be alone with this man. And with the flood of memories that accosted her came the same aching emotions from years before.

Unsure whether he was happy she had run into him, she tried to offer an easy way out. "If you want to be alone, I'll leave."

"Not this time." His voice, adamant and strong, calmed her.

She started to walk past him, but he hooked his hand around her elbow, keeping her firmly in place. "Talk to me."

She didn't want him to touch her again, because she knew from the heated flutter in her stomach that she'd fall into his arms at the first opportunity.

"Why didn't you tell me you were leaving?" he asked, his tone accusatory.

"I'm not going anywhere," she replied, deliberately misunderstanding.

"I meant fifteen years ago."

She gazed over his shoulder before answering. "It was after the trouble with the break-in. My father made the decision to leave. He came home one night, said we were leaving, and in just a few days we were gone. I didn't know how to contact you."

"Right," he chuckled bitterly, letting her go. "We didn't have a phone."

She gently broke from his hold and walked to the

steps of the landing to sit down, needing to stay out of his reach. She melted when he touched her—couldn't think straight. Right now she couldn't afford that. They needed to talk, to get things out into the open. "I felt bad, but the move was devastating for me. I didn't want to go, but, I didn't have a vote in the decision. Dad was firm." She folded her hands in her lap. "I wanted to let you know."

The light at the end of the alley turned his angled profile into a shadowed silhouette. His proud chin bespoke an arrogance Casey knew was a cover to hide his hurt.

"What do you really want, Ty?"

Her question must have thrown him off. His eyes narrowed. "What do you mean?"

"What do you want out of life?" She smiled. "When we were kids we used to talk about the future. Do you remember that?"

"Yeah. I do." Ty shifted his stance, crunching pebbles with his boots. "You and Mike were the only people I told those dreams to. And you always encouraged me. I appreciated that."

"Ty, you were bound for success, even back then. Bonnie told me about your scholarship to Georgia Tech. I was proud of you."

He hooked his thumbs in the belt loops of his jeans. "Ruby Sue was pretty happy, too. I was the first one in the family to go to college. Then Gabe and Marilyn followed." He stared up at the stars. "Seems we all got what we wanted. Respectability."

"You sound disappointed."

He turned his gaze to her. "Not for the example I

set for my brother and sister. I'd do whatever I could for them."

"They know that."

He shrugged his shoulders and braced his foot against the building. "I had to set the example. My mother was less than discreet when she went out looking for men. I guess my father leaving us took too much out of her. She didn't know how to cope. That's a burden we've all had to carry."

"Maybe it's time to let go of the past. She can't hurt your family anymore."

"She can if we follow in her footsteps."

Casey tilted her head. "What do you mean?"

With a heavy sigh, he said, "Marilyn thinks she needs to keep selling and making money, at the expense of a real life. I keep asking her, when is enough money enough?

"Then there's Gabe. Ever since Cindy died, it's like he's crawled into the grave with her. I can't help him with that kind of hurt. Not right now."

Casey's heart broke at the despair in his voice. "Are you trying to say you see some type of pattern in your family?"

"I guess. It seems we just can't get our acts together."

Casey squeezed her fingers tight to keep from reaching out to comfort him. They needed to talk, not make physical contact. She knew his confiding in her was difficult, but the fact that he'd taken that step meant he might be willing to let himself heal.

"I had a teacher tell me once that there comes a time in our lives when we have to stop the mistakes that make a family dysfunctional. Cut off the past and decide that the future will be positive. If you chose right now to change your attitude, I bet it would help the dilemmas of your brother and sister. It's obvious they look up to you, Ty. Maybe you need to take the first step."

He said nothing, just continued to stare out into the night surrounding them.

"You told me about your dreams to be a big builder, your hopes about settling in Paineville, with the respect of the community. You achieved all that, but in the past year your life has changed radically. So I'm asking, what do you want?"

"This very instant or for the long haul?"

"Let's start simple. What do you want right now?"

"To kiss you again."

Casey gasped, the sound loud and sharp in the silence following his words. She regained her composure and asked, "Why?"

Ty pushed from the wall and strolled toward her. "I want to relive that night fifteen years ago."

She stood, intending to slip past him and escape. But then his hand reached out and grabbed hers, pulling her to him. She froze, blood pounding in her ears. She wanted this, but dreaded it at the same time.

His grasp relaxed, but he still held her firm. The message in his eyes was clear—she wasn't going anywhere until this was settled. In agonizing slow motion, Ty lowered his head. His lips hovered over hers until she couldn't stand it any longer. Moving just slightly, she brought her lips to his.

The memory of that long-ago kiss faded in the explosive reality of this time and place. The twinkle of the stars, the musky evening scent, even the chirps of crickets faded into insignificance. She was in Ty's arms. Before tonight, she never admitted to herself that she had dreamed of a reunion such as this. She'd never forgotten him or the impact he had had on future relationships in her life. All men had paled in comparison to him. She'd come full circle, returning to the man who had captured her young heart that night so long ago. Only now he had the power to destroy the fragile rekindling of love. She prayed he wouldn't do that.

"Maybe this isn't a good idea," she murmured against his lips.

"It's the best idea I've had in ages," he whispered.

He tugged her closer to him just as the first crack of fireworks invaded the quiet night. Suddenly fearful of totally losing her heart to him, she stepped back. His past had too strong a hold on him. They both needed time to see where this crazy attraction would lead them. And how open they were to a commitment.

She spoke, breathess. "Ty, we need to be on even ground here. I don't want to depend on you, then have you take off if things get serious."

He ran a hand through his hair and rested his foot on the first step beside him. Waiting for him to say something, Casey looked into the sky. It was illuminated by flashes. Because they were behind the building, though, she couldn't completely see the colorful explosions.

"Do you want me to make some sort of commitment to you, Casey?" His voice seemed tired and faraway.

Reaching out to lay her hand on his arm, she could feel his tension. What could she say? Yes. Make me happy. Even at the expense of your happiness?

She wasn't that selfish, even though she wanted him more than he'd ever know. "Not until you're ready."

After an interminably long few seconds, he set his foot back on the ground and took her hand, leading her from behind the building to the outskirts of the park. From there they had a clear view of the light show, which was as harmless as fireflies compared to the bursts of emotion in her stomach.

He slipped his hand around her waist and she rested her head against his shoulder. Neither spoke, but she felt a change in him. Occasionally he would brush his lips over her hair, but he didn't try to pursue anything more.

"When we were kids planning our futures," he said, quiet but firm, "I kinda figured you'd be there. I never imagined you'd leave like you did. It threw me."

Casey felt tears sting her eyes. "I never knew you felt that way."

"But the past has made me what I am. I can't promise that I'll be there for you. I can't even promise myself any kind of future. I guess what I'm trying to say is that even though I don't know where I'm going, I need you to be here for me."

Heavy tears slid from underneath Casey's lids. What would he need her for? As an emotional sounding board? To be a good friend? She didn't ask. Because now she knew the truth.

They wanted different things. She wanted a home and family with someone reliable. He didn't know where he'd be after he finished the work on Casey's barn.

Chapter Eight

Ty yanked on the barn door behind Casey's house a good three times before it gave. As he dragged the door over the dry soil, the hinges squeaked and dust puffed up from the ground.

Light streaked in through the grimy windows. Ty stepped into the center of the structure, his contractor's mind kicking into overdrive. The square yardage of the building would give Casey plenty of room to store her merchandise. It was up to him to design a spacious working area.

He headed back to the truck, his step heavy. His conversation with Casey at the close of the Founder's Day celebration weighed on him. Since then they'd successfully avoided each other. It had been days since the parade, but he still couldn't shake his troubled thoughts.

He reached into the cab and grabbed hold of a pad

and pencil, then returned to the building, making notes and taking measurements. Before leaving Atlanta and basically turning the business over to his partner, he hadn't realized how much he had missed the manual labor. Now it was all coming back to him. The excitement of handling that new job. The feeling of well-being when the project was completed.

He shook his head. Casey's positive attitude mumbo-jumbo was beginning to rub off on him.

About a half hour later, Ty heard a vehicle in the driveway. He walked outside and squinted into the bright afternoon sun. To his surprise he saw Mike Post hopping out of his truck and approaching him.

"Casey told me you were working here." His gaze ran over the barn, then the house. "Didn't think you'd ever come back to this old place again."

"Marilyn talked me into it."

Mike grinned. "That girl always knew how to pull at you. How's your sister doing?"

"Making lots of money in the real estate game. She thinks she's happy."

"You think otherwise?"

"I've seen the circles under her eyes."

"Ahh. Enough said."

Ty crossed his arms over his chest. "So, what brings you out here?"

"Casey mentioned that she had plans to store some of my work in the future. Just wanted to check out her facility."

Chuckling, Ty swept his arm toward the barn. "After you."

Mike walked past him into the dark interior and

came to an abrupt halt just over the threshold. "Was she kidding me?"

Ty followed. "No. I'm starting work to clean this place up. Don't worry, the walls are safe and in good shape. The roof doesn't leak. It's just a matter of building some office space and fixing up decent storage area."

"You always were good at seeing the big picture."

"Yeah, and missing things going on right under my nose." Ty cast one last glimpse around the barn, then turned to walk back outside with Mike.

"You've got to stop beating yourself up over Sabrina."

"So I've heard."

They stopped beneath a tall oak. Ty inhaled the hot summer air and the sweet grass. It calmed him until Mike spoke.

"She called me the other day. First time in months."

Ty narrowed his eyes and waited for the news. He wouldn't ask. He couldn't.

"As usual, she wanted information. Thought my ties here might keep me up-to-date on what's going on. Since no one is willing to talk to her, she's in a snit. Marilyn is supposed to be working on the deal for that shop in the town square. They've run into some trouble."

His eyebrow raised. "Really? Marilyn mentioned something about that but didn't give details."

"Sabrina got word that the owner changed his mind about selling. She's got some deal in the works with a big-time company so she's furious because her plans are going south. I guess the owner wants more money and John doesn't want to pay."

"So what's the big deal? John's got money. If he wanted Sabrina, he had to know she'd spend it for him."

He shrugged. "I didn't get all the details. Sabrina was upset because Marilyn can't get ahold of the owner."

"And Marilyn's up to her bottled blond hair on this one. Seems like everyone is going to lose out."

Ty leaned against the tree trunk, the sun-warmed bark scratching his arm. "John should cut his losses now and make a run for it."

"Yeah, but you know Sabrina's stubborn streak. She won't give up that easily."

How he remembered. From the time Sabrina decided to pursue him, she'd been relentless. His male ego had loved the attention.

Yeah, he remembered how she could be when she wanted her way. Didn't look like she'd get it this time. He allowed himself a half smile.

Mike stared at him. "I know that look."

Ty took a deep breath and decided to confide in his friend. "I own the buildings in town."

Mike let out a low whistle. "How long?"

"Five years. When I started making money Ruby Sue talked me into investing in this town. I started a corporation to keep my ownership a secret. The folks in this town already know too much about my life. I wanted privacy and time to see how the deal would work out. If it messes up Sabrina's plans, then it'll finally pay off."

"In revenge?"

Ty shrugged.

"Does Casey know?"

Ty shook his head, ignoring the sinking feeling in the pit of his stomach. "Only the lawyers. And now you."

"Casey's not going to be happy."

"I know." He swallowed hard. He'd hate the day when she looked at him in disappointment.

He'd been less than honest when she had asked about his firm doing the renovations. He should have set her straight, but it was too late now.

"How long will the barn renovation take?" Mike asked, pulling Ty from his thoughts.

"I figure a couple of weeks should take care of it. Definitely by the end of the summer."

"Then what?"

"I move on to another job."

Mike looked down at his work boots, then back to Ty. "You and Casey work things out?"

"Why, did she say something?"

"No. She just seemed kind of quiet today. Didn't really want to talk about you."

Ty frowned. Why should her reaction bother him? Didn't he tell her he couldn't promise her any kind of commitment? It wasn't like he was stringing her along. He'd told her the truth.

The fact that they'd remained friends was great, but the idea of getting to know her on a deeper level scared him. He didn't want to have expectations, only to be disappointed. No, they were better off just where they were, in an emotional limbo.

"Mike, we're friends. I enjoy being with her."

"Okay." He pulled a key ring from his pants pocket. "But from the look of that guy who came in to visit her at the store before I left, I'd say you have some competition, buddy. Had on a Wall Street suit, salon-styled hair, the works. But, hey." He shrugged. "If you're just friends. . . ."

As Mike sauntered out to his truck, Ty bit his tongue to refrain from shouting any questions after him. Casey's life was her own, just as his was his own. If some guy pursued her, he had no claims to stop him.

So why did he feel like he'd been kicked in the gut?

"Miles, I've told you twenty times, I'm not coming back to work for you. Not under any circumstances."

"Casey, you'll get a *major* pay raise."

"Don't need it."

"Major perks. A new car. New territory."

"With lots of *major* work. Do you realize how long it took me to build my client base before you gave it away? I'm not working that hard for you again."

Miles had the good grace to look embarrassed. "Please, Casey. My bosses really want you back."

Ahh, she thought. *The real reason you're here. To save your own hide.*

"Miles, you're wasting your time. I'm happy here. I have no intention of giving up the store."

As if seeing the place for the first time, he glanced around, light reflecting off his designer-framed glasses. "But you're so far away from everything."

"I like it here, Miles. This is home."

He looked at her as if she'd sprouted horns. Then he scanned her outfit and grimaced. "There's not even a decent clothing store around here."

She laughed. "So, I have to travel to get to a mall. It doesn't bother me." Nor did her lack of power suit and toe-pinching pumps. She felt more free—more alive—wearing a blouse, shorts, and sandals.

"Casey, you're used to a high-profile job. Surely this store can't compare with that?"

"Yes, it can. I own this place. No one can take it away from me," she emphasized. "I like being the boss."

Miles shook his head, purposely pretending he didn't hear her barb. He pulled a card and an expensive pen from his jacket pocket. "Here is my cell phone number. Think about my offer and call me. I'm sure you'll realize what a sweet deal this is. Then you'll want your old job back."

Casey sighed. He didn't have a clue as to what she wanted. Now that she thought back on it, she realized he never really had. She wanted to kick herself for the time she had wasted with him.

Taking the card from his outstretched hand, she plastered a smile on her face. "Thank you for stopping by, Miles."

He nodded, obviously encouraged by her smile. "Call me. I've missed you." The uncharacteristic waver in his voice almost touched her heart.

She would have believed him if she hadn't noticed the calculating gleam in his eye. He knew how to play her. That's why she'd given in to him so many times before.

But not today. "Good-bye."

It didn't take five minutes before Casey filed the card. "Right, I'll call you," she muttered, dropping the card in the wastebasket.

Half an hour later, Bonnie arrived, children in tow. "Sorry I'm late, Case. Chuck got a call from work and had to go in. He can't watch the kids and my mother-in-law isn't home." She ushered the children into the back room. "I thought maybe we could put them to work here."

"Actually, we could use the help. We just received a delivery today, so they can sort through it for us. How does that sound?"

Bonnie rolled up her sleeves. "Tommy. Lindsay. We have work to do."

The children nodded eagerly and helped their mother tear back the cardboard lid and pull out the bubble wrap.

Casey watched, smiling at the children. An ache in the vicinity of her heart pressed on her diaphragm. Bonnie had sent pictures of her children from the moment they were born. Tommy, thirteen, was growing into a young man. Lindsay still had the little-girl look of a nine-year-old, but that would change soon.

Miles's visit drove home her recent desire for a family of her own. She hadn't dwelled on it in her previous job. She'd worked so many hours with so many days on the road, a family hadn't made sense.

But now she lived in a small town and had a home, a place with lots of room for children and visiting relatives. A big back-yard for cookouts. A gazebo for romantic nights under the summer stars. All she had to do was find someone to share that dream with her. Perhaps Ty would be that man.

Don't count on it, her inner voice warned. She closed her eyes and leaned against the display counter. Her brain knew that, but her heart told her not to give up yet.

Their relationship had been subdued these past days, but at least he hadn't completely closed the door. How she'd prayed that he'd overcome his emotionally crippling past. In her naïveté, she thought that maybe she could be the one to get him to love again. But his resistance was too strong.

So your love has to be stronger.

Her lids flew open. Love? When had she fallen in love? Probably back in high school when that determined senior asked for her help to pass English Lit.

She sighed. So many years had gone by, so many obstacles stood in their way. Not only his past, but her desire to succeed. She didn't want a man in her life if he would hold her back. She'd been there already. She wanted a man who would share in her success. And until Ty straightened his own life out, he wouldn't be there for her. They both knew that.

The children's laughter filled the store and Casey's doubts resurfaced. Maybe coming home wasn't such a good idea. She never would have missed what she left behind if she hadn't come back, right?

"Great idea," Bonnie remarked, as she joined Casey at the counter. "The kids really like to help."

"Let's make sure we pay them before you leave. Cheap labor is hard to find."

"Cheap labor would be not paying them at all and

giving them a hamburger for lunch instead. But I get the idea." Bonnie grinned as she flipped through a stack of invoices. "Speaking of laborers, how's Ty?"

Casey rolled her eyes. Now that everyone knew he was working at her place, it was the only question people asked her. "He's okay, I guess. I'm not his personal secretary."

"Ohh, touchy."

Casey held up her hand. "Let's change the subject."

"Something wrong?" Bonnie persisted.

Casey's thoughts scrambled. Should she confide in her cousin? It had to be better than keeping it all inside. But did she even want to put her doubts into words?

"You've been kinda quiet since the other night. Ty didn't hurt you, did he?"

"No. He's been painfully honest from the start. I guess I just let myself think we could build something together. I was wrong."

Bonnie pursed her lips, laying a comforting hand over Casey's. "I don't want to say I told you so, but everyone knows he's a mess."

"You warned me, I know. I thought . . . maybe I could be the one to change all that." She shook her head at the dismal results. "Crazy, I know."

Bonnie squeezed her hand. "No, caring. Just one of the many wonderful qualities Ty's missing out on while he hides like a turtle in his shell."

Casey laughed. "Thanks for the support."

"Hey, that's what I'm here for."

A loud voice came from the back room. "Mom, we're finished. What can we do now?"

"Duty calls." Bonnie hurried off to give instructions.

Casey roamed the aisles, absently straightening items and admiring the more complex works of art. She reached the front of the store and stopped.

Mike Post's carvings caught her imagination. He breathed life into the wood, allowing her to feel freedom along with his soaring bird, or pride in the way an eagle surveyed all from his perch.

Power and emotion.

The strength reminded her of Ty.

She ran her fingers over the warm wood. Such talent.

She tried to remember Mike from their high school days. He'd been athletic and popular with the girls, but now, after all the years, she could only picture him running around with Ty.

Ty had dominated her thoughts then as he did now. Once again the idea that she shouldn't have come back to Paineville clouded her thoughts.

Until she glanced around the store. Her store. She swore no man would make her lose sight of her goals. And that included Ty Banner.

Around twelve-thirty the next day, Ty decided to take a break. He'd been working steadily all morning, keeping his mind blank and his hands busy. He'd just stepped out of the barn when a white, four-door sedan eased up the driveway. The driver halted alongside Ty's truck and parked, giving Ty a better view of the car.

Expensive.

The door opened and a tall, blond man emerged. He glanced around as he pushed his glasses up the bridge of his nose and smoothed back his sleek hair. His searching stopped when his gaze met Ty's. His eyebrows rose. Straightening his tie, he sauntered over.

Ty grinned, noting the way this guy wore his suit as a statement: Look at me, I've got it all and I know it. Geez, where did he come from?

Ty crossed his arms over his worn T-shirt, tucked into his equally worn jeans. The irony wasn't lost on him.

"Excuse me. I'm looking for Casey Hudson."

"She's not home." Ty grinned. "You must have missed her. I think she went to her store."

The man frowned, then caught himself and snapped his fingers. "Every time I've been by the store she's gone. I thought I'd catch her at home."

"She's like that. You never know what to expect."

"And, ah, how would you know?"

"I work for her."

The expression on the stranger's face went blank for a moment, then registered the idea that Ty's presence here now made sense. How else would Ty know about her? "Who should I say came by?"

"Miles Sanborn." He extended his hand and flashed his smarmiest smile.

Deciding to be gentlemanly, Ty shook his hand. "Ty Banner."

"And you work for Casey?"

"That's right. I'm remodeling the barn."

"For . . . ?"

He shrugged. "You'll have to ask her that."

Miles glanced at the barn, then turned and looked at the house. "I don't expect she'll need your help much longer."

"Really?" This guy really had Ty's interest now.

"Yes," he said, as he pushed his glasses again and regarded Ty. "I was her boss before she got the ludicrous idea to embrace small-town living. Once she gets tired of this quaint idea, she'll decide to come back to the corporation. It's not the first time she's left us, only to come back."

"Really?"

"Sure. She thought she might strike out in a different market, but the company folded so she came back to me. She'll do the same once her little store begins to bore her."

"I don't think so."

Miles looked suspicious. "And how would you know?"

"You'd be surprised what people tell the help."

Miles sized him up again and Ty got the distinct impression he was lacking in the other man's view. It almost made him laugh out loud.

"I can't image Casey confiding in you."

"But she confides in you?" Ty shot back.

"Of course." He hesitated a heartbeat. "I guess she didn't tell you that we were involved."

That explained Casey's evasiveness on the subject. "I guess she doesn't tell me everything."

An uncertain look momentarily flashed across Miles's face. "I'm surprised she didn't say anything. I've been in and out of town for a couple of days now."

"Must have slipped her mind."

Miles chuckled, then jammed his hands in his pants pocket and turned to examine the house. Ty couldn't imagine how Casey had fallen into a relationship with someone so unlike her, unless they shared the same business ambitions.

This guy oozed false charm. Granted, he was fairly good-looking, but Ty figured Casey was fooled by his charm and blatant attention. He was the consummate businessman. Schmoozing came second nature to guys like him.

And after years with Sabrina, he could spot a phony in a second. Casey was as honest as they came.

Honest in her concern for him. Honest in her physical attraction for him. It was enough to go to a guy's head.

Ty started the conversation again. "She didn't mention a boyfriend."

Miles cleared his throat. "We took a break after she resigned. Once she comes to her senses, we'll get together again."

Somehow Ty doubted that. But that little nagging voice in the back of his mind took pleasure in tormenting him. *Why shouldn't she go back to him? You have nothing permanent to offer.*

"So, you expect her to take her old job back." Ty's words were a statement.

"Any day now."

"And how many times has she said no?"

"I beg your pardon?"

"Casey has too much at stake to give up the store." The man looked concerned now, less sure of himself. "She can't pass up my offer. It's much too generous."

But Ty hoped she would. He couldn't imagine her working for this pompous guy, let alone having a relationship with him.

"If I were you, I'd take out an ad. She's not coming back."

"And what makes you so sure about that?"

"Because we're seeing each other now."

The sound of tires on rock and dirt turned both men from their conversation. Casey pulled up behind the pickup and jumped out of the car, moving quickly toward them. Even from the distance between them, Ty could read the distress on her face.

Miles lifted his chin. "We'll just see about that."

The male line had been drawn.

Casey's gaze went from one man to the other and panic consumed her. What if Miles led Ty to believe she was leaving? Would he see it as another betrayal? Ty's polite smile gave away no clue as to what he might be thinking.

"Miles, what're you doing here?"

The man she once considered important in her life took a step between her and Ty, his self-assured smile grating on her nerves. "Waiting for you. We have a lot to talk about."

She looked around him. Ty had his arms crossed over his chest, his gaze piercing hers. "Would you give us a few minutes?"

"Sure thing." Ty winked before disappearing into the barn.

Placing her hands on her hips, Casey turned her

attention to Miles. Despite the summer heat and lack of elegant surroundings, he still chose to wear a suit. She almost smiled. At least some things never changed. "I think you'd better tell me why you're here."

"Let's go into the house."

"I don't think so. You aren't welcome here. This is my place and I won't have you dictating what I do."

He held up his hands. "Sorry."

"Just tell me what you want."

"You know what I want. Take the job."

"I've already told you no. How can I make it any clearer?"

"You don't expect me to believe you're happy here?"

"I don't care if you believe me or not. It's over between us, professionally and personally."

Miles lost his usual cool as he pointed to the barn. "And I suppose dating that Neanderthal in there isn't just a passing phase."

Her brow wrinkled. "Who said I was dating him?"

"He did."

Ty actually admitted they were dating? Casey felt warm with pleasure. She'd question him about that later, but right now she had to deal with Miles.

And make her point so he'd go away.

"Unlike you, I don't use people. Ty and I have a real friendship and for your information, yes, it may be more. So get back in your fancy car and find some other flunky to fill your slot. I'm not, and never will be, interested."

Miles scowled at her, taking a few steps before he

turned on his heel. "You'll be sorry. I won't give you your job back, even if you come crawling."

She practically smirked. "Yes you will, if your boss tells you to."

His shoulders pushed back, Miles straightened his jacket and tugged on the hem. He opened his mouth to speak, then turned and stomped back to his car. Casey stepped back as Miles slammed the car into reverse. Bits of grass and gravel shot up as the car turned and sped down the driveway.

Casey massaged her temples. A headache was coming on and she hadn't even confronted Ty yet.

Taking a few minutes to catch her breath, Casey inhaled the fresh, woodsy-scented air. She then pushed aside the worn wooden barn door and walked into the room littered with two-by-fours, tools, and sawhorses. The radio blared country music. Ty started to hammer. The pain in her head kept time to each strike on the nail.

"Could you turn that noise off?" she shouted over the music.

Ty turned and grinned. "That's not noise, darlin'. That's life."

"Well, I've had enough of life lately. Can you turn it down?"

Ty's eyes zeroed in on her. He stepped down from the ladder to turn the radio off. The sudden silence washed over her and she felt her shoulders relax. Miles's visit had stretched her nerves to the max.

"Tough day?" Ty asked, tossing a bunch of nails into a box.

"I've had better." She waited for him to mention

Miles, but he continued to observe her. "I guess you want to know about my guest?"

Ty raised one eyebrow. "Is that what he was? Got the impression he was an old flame."

Casey felt herself flush. Miles was so underhanded. He probably saw Ty as a threat and decided to falsely inflate his position in her life. "To be honest, whatever he was, it was short-lived."

Ty propped his hip against a sawhorse and crossed his tanned arms over his chest. "And I thought my taste was bad."

She grinned. "He wasn't exactly my shining hour."

"So, you want to tell me what happened?"

The grin faded. "I worked for years to assemble a large and profitable client base. Miles always praised me about my work; of course now I realize that I made him look good to his bosses. We dated. It never really developed into anything."

She shook her head sadly. "I guess I settled. The relationship was easy. We had work in common, and after work we had the same friends in common. I thought things would work out. They didn't."

Ty uncrossed his arms and placed his hands at his sides. "What happened?"

Casey looked away. "I dropped by his apartment one night after getting back into town a day early. I landed a new account and wanted to celebrate." She swallowed, surprised that she could still feel any sort of hurt over what Miles had done. After all, he was a rat. "He was entertaining a new employee, another woman. Needless to say, he was as surprised to see me as I was to see her. After a not-so-friendly discussion, the woman informed me that Miles had given her my territory.

"At first I thought she was blowing smoke, until I went to the office the following morning. Sure enough, he'd done just as she said. In return, he wanted me to start from scratch in a whole new area of the country. That meant endless hours of work, countless days of traveling, and making new connections all over again."

"Didn't you try to explain to his superiors?"

"There wasn't much point. I'd done such a good job for them that the powers-that-be decided a new territory was just what I needed. To expand their pockets." She lifted her chin. "So I quit on the spot."

Ty smiled. "Good for you."

"Yeah. So that's how I ended up here. I called Bonnie to cry on her shoulder and she talked me into a visit. I figured if I was going to work long hours, I might as well do something I loved." She waved her hand over the expanse of the barn.

"So you're not gonna take the job?"

"Would it matter to you if I did?"

"Yeah, actually it would."

The pleasant glow returned. "Well, the answer is no, I won't be going back. But he can't get it through his thick skull that I'm happy here."

"Yeah, well, he doesn't get it. There aren't too many jobs around here that require a designer suit."

Spying a plastic milk crate on the ground, Casey turned it over and sat down. She stretched out her legs and glanced up at Ty, spying the heated light in his eyes before he turned away.

When he remained silent she asked, "So, we're dating now?"

"He told you."

"Yes. Is it true?"

Ty ran his hand over the back of his neck. "I wanted to make the guy jealous. Hoped he'd leave you alone. It just sorta came out." He averted his eyes. "Think he'll leave town now?"

She sighed in disappointment. So much for her alluring female magnetism. "Eventually. I can't make 'no' any clearer than I have. He'll just have to accept it. I'm settled here. Or at least as long as I have the store."

Ty stopped in the motion of picking up his electrical saw. "What do you mean?"

"The rumors have started up again. A major chain store to put of us out of business."

A dark shadow passed over his face. "Where did you get that information?"

She shrugged. "I didn't get it, Bonnie did. Everyone is really worried."

"It won't happen."

"How can you be so sure? No one even knows who the owner is."

Ty walked over and hunkered down beside her. "Don't worry so much about the future."

"I have to. If I have to close the store I'll lose everything. And if the store fails, maybe the catalog idea won't fly and then I'd have to take Miles up on his offer."

"Shh." Ty hovered close. "I said, don't worry."

"You seem so sure about nothing bad happening. I'm afraid I don't have the same faith."

"Casey, you're doing a great job. The store is a success. Don't tempt fate."

"I try not to, but lately I feel like everything is falling apart."

"What else could possibly be wrong?"

"There's always the chance that you might leave," she said quietly.

Ty leaned back on heels. "Why do you say that?"

"I see how you close up when we talk about the future. Am I wrong?"

"I haven't decided one way or the other."

Pushing aside all her problems, Casey gently ran her palm over Ty's cheek. He lifted her from the crate and held her firmly in his embrace. He kissed her, soft and reassuring. The type of kiss she imagined a couple sharing when they came together to confront an uncertain future. Since that was the case here, it made the time between them that much more bittersweet.

"Casey, I need to tell you this. You make me feel more than I ever wanted to," he whispered, his lips close to hers. "All I know is when I'm with you I want to kiss you upside down and sideways." With that, he covered her lips with his. Until now, Ty's kisses had been sweet, leaving her longing for more. But now she felt a deep hunger in both of them. And she wished it would last forever.

A lump closed off her throat and she broke away from the kiss. Ty stayed close to her but didn't say a word. She inhaled his male scent—one of hard work—

exclusively Ty. He traced his finger over her lips as he released her.

"I—I, um, have to go up to the house," Casey murmured.

Ty nodded, his eyes dark. "I wish I could help you."

"How about agreeing to a future with me?"

He faltered.

"I didn't think so."

Chapter Nine

Much to Casey's surprise, Ty called the following weekend to invite her to a family party. She wanted to decline, but when he told her it was Emily's birthday and the young girl wanted to see her, Casey couldn't resist. Besides, her will power regarding Ty grew less and less every day.

She dressed casually—a print challis skirt and matching top, with flat sandals with laces that tied around her ankles. She put on makeup, fluffed her hair, and waited for Ty to pick her up.

With time to kill, she sat down at the kitchen table to look over her list of mail-order details before requests came in about the catalogue. She figured that Ty would be finished with the barn by the end of next week. She had the merchandise lined up, and once it was shipped to her she could inventory the stock right there. Then the last phase of her dream would be up and running.

While she was pleased with her accomplishment, a sense of fulfillment eluded her. She should be happy to see her dream unfolding. So what was missing? Had her initial dream changed into something else? Someone else?

She groaned, not wanting to face that answer. Here she was, trying to convince herself that she wanted to prove something to Ty, yet he continued to push her away. Maybe what she refused to see was that Ty wasn't the right man for her.

Her thoughts faded as she heard a vehicle move up the driveway. She peeked out the window and saw Ty's battered pickup.

Sighing, she picked up her purse and Emily's gift. *By the end of next week summer would be nearly over and the barn would be finished.* Is that how much time she had left with him? Maybe that's why he wouldn't confide any of his secrets in her. Instead, he'd just move away from the small town that held such painful memories for him. And leave her behind.

She squared her shoulders. If he left, she would be fine. She had her work. Her friends. Her interests. Yeah, she thought. That would keep her warm at night.

Still, she decided to enjoy whatever time they had left. Whether he left, or they decided not to stay together, a decision would have to be made soon. She only hoped it was the right one.

The doorbell rang just as she reached for the knob. Ty stood on the porch, looking heavenly in faded jeans and, surprisingly, a new T-shirt.

She nodded at him. "This *must* be a special occasion. New shirt?"

He grinned. "Ruby Sue got tired of my wardrobe. She bought me a bunch of new shirts, then invaded the trailer, stole my old shirts, and burned them."

Casey's eyebrows rose. "You're kidding."

He held up his hand. "I'm not lying. She did that once back in high school. I had to hide my leather jacket until she forgot about it." He laughed. "You'd think by now I'd take her threats more seriously."

Casey locked the door behind her, wondering just what she was getting herself into by visiting his family.

"Don't worry, it's safe. Today she's all excited about Emily. Had to have this big shindig so that friends Emily only sees once a year could visit." He paused and grinned. "And the fact that I invited you."

"I take it that doesn't happen often?"

"Since we're the talk of the town, I figured I should ask you," he teased.

He helped her into the cab, then jumped in on his side. "I have a favor to ask."

She looked over at him and noticed the eager expression on his face. "What is it?"

"I need to get a present for Emily."

"Nothing like waiting till last minute," she murmured.

"I know. I don't know what a girl her age likes. I thought maybe we could stop in town and pick something out for her. Together."

Casey's heart leapt and she hoped her voice sounded casual. "We could do that."

"Great." He started the ignition and headed out of the driveway. "So, what do you get an eleven-year-old anyway? A doll, maybe?"

"I think she's getting too old for that. She's at a point where she wants to start being treated like a grown-up." She thought about her own childhood for a minute. "How about a CD?"

"I don't know what groups she likes."

"Clothes, then."

He grimaced. "I haven't got a clue about girl's clothes."

She smirked. "That's why you have me."

He glanced at her, amusement twinkling in his dark eyes. "I knew there was a reason."

They arrived at the square and Ty parked near the only upscale clothing town in store. Once inside, Casey browsed through a rack of clothing, her forehead creased in concentration. Ty remained by the door, ready to bolt if any of the guys he knew walked by.

Nothing caught Casey's fancy. Or at least what she thought a young girl would like. Trying to hide her concern, she went to the salesperson for advice. "Do you have anything, um, trendy, for an eleven-year-old?"

The middle-aged woman smiled. "Actually, I just got a shipment yesterday that might interest you. I haven't had a chance to put it out yet, but you're welcome to look." She stepped close and whispered to Casey behind her hand. "He looks worried."

"This is a present for his niece. He hasn't got a clue."

The woman chuckled. "Thank goodness he has you."

That was the second time she had heard that phrase today. Should she take it to heart? She wished with all her soul that it was true.

Following the woman to the sales counter, Casey immediately spied an outfit that Emily would love. A cute pullover with embroidered flowers matched a pair of denim jeans styled in the current fashion. On the shelf behind the counter was a denim hat with the same flowers stitched on the folded brim of the hat. Matched up with a necklace, it would delight any girl.

Casey picked out the correct size and called to Ty. "My work is done here. Pay the lady."

He picked up the shirt. "Looks kinda small."

"It's the style."

"Remind me to never have girls." He pulled out his wallet and handed over the cash.

Casey tried to ignore his slip. Instead she concentrated on the task at hand.

"If you want, I can gift wrap it for you," the woman said.

Ty handed her an extra ten-dollar bill. "I'd be grateful."

The woman's cheeks grew pink at his display of charm. Casey rolled her eyes and walked away. He knew he had an effect on women. Rascal.

She left Ty with the gushing clerk and wandered around the store. To her dismay, she ended up in the baby department. Pastel, soft, frilly dresses with matching booties and bonnets snagged her attention. One display showed off bib overalls with a train embroidered on the front. Little sleepers and play outfits hung on a round rack.

A catch in Casey's throat unnerved her. Since settling into small-town life she'd thought more and more about a family every day. The idea of "someday" seemed to be fast approaching, and seeing these darling clothes made her longing even more tangible. Would she ever have children of her own? A husband who adored her as much as she loved him?

"Okay, Casey, let's go."

Feeling a large hand touch the small of her back, she spun around, not realizing how close Ty was. His look was questioning until he glanced past her to the baby clothes. The light in his eyes dimmed, and she felt her stomach dip in regret. That look said it all. He didn't want a wife and family. She realized that was another point in the long list of things that kept them apart. It also served as a sharp reminder that as much as she wanted it, Ty was all wrong for her.

"Emily is going to love the outfit," she said with false cheer, taking his arm and leading him from the shop. "Her favorite uncle's gift will be a big hit."

She felt Ty relax and hoped he wouldn't realize the depth of her yearning. He held her heart in the palm of his hand and didn't even know it.

Ruby Sue made a big production of Ty's arrival with Casey. The woman acted as though he had never brought a date home. Well, he hadn't, but the old woman didn't have to act so darn smug. It got under his skin when Ruby Sue tossed him that "we'll see how this turns out" look.

Casey seemed to fit right in with his family. He watched in awe as she called out cheerful greetings and gave her attention to the hostess. Sabrina never did that.

As much as he'd promised himself not to make comparisons, it was obvious that Casey was completely different from his ex-fiancée, at least with his family. He was still waiting for the shoe to drop about the business coming first, but for now Ty began to relax. He decided to stop comparing Casey to Sabrina and to really enjoy getting to know who Casey was. She never failed to surprise him, and he was getting used to that.

Emily ran up to Casey and hugged her. Casey seemed surprised at first, but then returned the hug with enthusiasm. Gabe had her engaged in conversation before Emily ran away to show off another gift to her friends. Ruby Sue plunked an iced tea in Casey's hand and they chatted like long lost friends.

Ty laughed. The poor woman was being bombarded by the Banner family. Then, suddenly, Ty felt like he was on the outside looking in.

It was his own fault really. They always expected him to be moody. But Casey got to him. He had hesitated about asking her over today—after all, he'd all but told Casey they had no future. But Ruby Sue nagged him till he couldn't stand it another minute.

Deep down he had to admit he was pleased she'd agreed to come. He found himself wanting to be with her all the time. He liked talking to her. He liked hearing her opinions on things. He liked the way she stared at him like he was the only man on earth.

But he wasn't comfortable with the yearning he always saw on her face, like today at the clothing store. He might care about her—and care deeply—but he wasn't ready for the family scene. As much as he'd wanted a family at one time, Sabrina had knocked down that idea even before they were to be married, convincing him that they needed to establish themselves in business before taking on such a responsibility. He hadn't pushed the issue, and before long gave up on the idea completely. It only made him realize that maybe he wasn't the family type.

What if he couldn't stay married? Just like his father. What if he made a lousy parent? Like his mother. He was better off with no responsibilities. Then no one would get hurt. Not even him.

Gabe walked over and smacked him on the back. "Glad you brought Casey. Emily really likes her."

"Anything for my niece."

"What about for yourself?"

"I'm happy."

"Really? So, decided to get serious with Casey?"

"No, why would you think that?"

"Because you can't take your eyes off of her."

Ty groaned. "Guess I can't convince you anymore that we're just friends."

"You may be able to convince yourself, but what about Casey? Her feelings are written all over her face."

"I know."

"So, you gonna make her an honest woman?"

It was getting harder to just come out and say no.

But the fact remained that Casey needed a guy more suited to her needs.

Ty stood mute until Gabe gave a sad shake of his head.

"I guess I can take that as a no," Gabe said and sighed. "You should give it a try. She's worth it."

"Don't you think I know that?" Ty grumbled.

"Testy."

"Yeah, just like Mom got whenever Ruby Sue used give her the third degree."

Gabe's expression sobered. "Point taken."

Ty sighed. "Sorry, man. I didn't meant to jump all over you."

"I can take it, but I don't think Casey can. At least not for much longer."

Casey tried not to keep looking in Ty's direction as he and Gabe ended what looked to be a very intense discussion. But the bleak expression on Ty's face had her worried. She really hoped she wasn't the topic of conversation.

Ruby Sue took Casey's arm and they sauntered to a grouping of lawn chairs under a shady tree in the backyard. "He didn't used to be so guarded," Ruby Sue began.

Once seated, Casey sipped her tea. The day was cool, but her mouth was dry. Probably in anticipation of a not-so-distant future when Ty would leave her.

"He doesn't have to be now. I would never hurt him; he knows that." Casey felt comfortable opening up to the older woman.

"The boy isn't willin' to take a chance again. Much

as I'd like to see him settled down with someone nice like you, he still won't take the first step."

Casey stared into the woman's shrewd eyes, her spirits dropping. "So what should I do?" she asked, fighting off hot tears.

Ruby Sue shook her head. "To be honest, I wouldn't know what kind of advice to give you."

Casey sighed heavily, getting her emotions under control.

"I was married to Ty's grandaddy until the man up and died. And I haven't had any interest in another man since. I got a feelin' that you and I are from the same mold."

Casey grinned. "You're probably right about that."

"How long have you known my grandson?"

"Since high school."

Clearly that was news to Ruby Sue if her raised eyebrows were any indication. "That long? The boy never said a word."

"We were friends. We did homework together. Ran into each other at parties. Things like that. My parents decided to move the summer after Ty graduated high school. We left before I had a chance to tell him."

Ruby Sue nodded, not surprised. "I thought Ty had something on his mind but he wouldn't tell me. Or anyone."

The group of girls on the porch started giggling. Casey glanced over their way, regretting that she'd never spent summers like them. Gossiping about boys. Poring over magazines for the latest fashions and teen idols. Instead, she'd usually been alone.

"That was the summer Ty's mama left for good. I sure was glad he had college to run off to in the fall."

"You must be very proud of him."

Pride glistened in Ruby Sue's eyes. "More than he'll ever know." Uncomfortable with this show of emotion, Ruby Sue cleared her throat. "But the boy is acting like a horse's back end now."

Casey's eyes widened. "I beg your pardon?"

"Seems to me he should forget the past and move on. He's got a chance, doesn't he?"

Trying to ignore the woman's expectant gaze, Casey swallowed her iced tea. "Some people have a harder time getting over disappointment."

"His pride is hurt, that's all. He was dealt too much of that male ego than is good for him."

Casey laughed. "Yeah, he is pretty loaded in that department."

Conversation fell into a lull. Casey sipped her beverage, watching the family members all around her. The girls still shared secrets, Ty and Gabe were tossing a football. A Cadillac pulled up into the drive and Marilyn got out. She was dressed casually like everyone else, and stopped to visit the girls.

Ruby Sue broke the silence. "So do you two think you'll have kids?"

Casey spilled her tea and gasped. "Wh . . . what?"

"Well, it gives one cause to wonder. If you get hitched and all."

Casey knew, just knew, that her face glowed redder than at any other time in her life. Her brain ceased to work. The proverbial cat held her tongue. She felt like a complete idiot.

"I know my grandson. You two need to settle this thing once and for all."

Casey still couldn't speak. If she ran now, maybe she could make it off the property before anyone caught her.

Ruby Sue harumphed. "What could it hurt?"

"I . . . I don't know," Casey stammered.

"Hi, Gran." Marilyn kissed Ruby Sue's cheek. "Casey. How are the renovations coming?"

"Just great. Ty should be finishing the barn very soon."

Marilyn flashed her the sales smile. "So glad to hear it."

Ruby Sue narrowed her eyes at her granddaughter. "You know what you need? A husband and babies. That'd clear up that pinched look on your face."

Casey felt a touch of sympathy as she watched Marilyn choke.

Ruby Sue must desperately want more great-grandchildren. Casey realized how hard it must be on Ruby Sue to have three grandchildren, with no love lives, and Emily so far away.

"Gran, that would only make things worse. I need to work right now."

"Heaven forbid any of my grandchildren be happy." Ruby Sue rose from the chair, a regal matriarch taking leave of an unpleasant conversation. Casey hid the smile pulling at her lips.

"She's a drama queen," Marilyn drawled as she took the abandoned seat.

"It works," Casey replied. She looked at Marilyn and they burst out laughing.

"Let me guess. She has you and Ty walking down the aisle."

"Yes. And she tried the baby thing on me, too."

Marilyn rolled her eyes. "The woman has no scruples. Some things never change."

Casey looked over at the men playing ball. "How about your brothers?"

"Gabe hasn't been the same since Cindy died. If it weren't for Emily, I don't know how he'd cope. She keeps him sane."

"And on his toes, I imagine."

"Yeah. She's a handful. And then there's Ty."

"Ty?" Casey swallowed.

Marilyn grew contemplative. "He still won't talk about what happened. I guess his ego's really bruised. For someone as proud as Ty, Sabrina's betrayal cut deep."

"So I keep hearing."

"Don't give up, Casey. I think you'd really be good for him."

She tamped down any hopeful feelings and just shrugged. "That remains to be seen."

"I pushed him to date Sabrina. That's a mistake I wish I could take back. He's never come out and said he blames me, but I think he should."

"He made his own choice. No matter how much you might have encouraged him, he still had the final say in that department."

"It's funny. I really thought they had it together. I mean, I knew she was ambitious, but it seemed like they made a good team. Just goes to show how wrong you can be about things."

Casey looked over at the men again in time to catch Ty strolling toward them. Her heart beat a little faster, especially in light of the way his eyes caught and held hers.

"Finished with the girl talk?"

Marilyn stepped away. "I'll leave you two alone."

Ty grabbed Casey's hand and yanked her from the chair. "Don't worry about it. We're going for a walk."

"We are?" Her heart jumped into her throat.

His gaze held hers, steady. "Oh, yeah, we are."

He took her hand and led her into the seclusion of woods bordering the property. Tender pine needles formed a carpet as they passed under towering trees. The scent of damp earth lingered in the air. Mottled sunshine scattered along the path as Ty led her to a clearing.

"I assume you know where you're going?"

"I grew up in these woods, darlin'. There's no way I could get lost."

"Maybe not here," Casey muttered, thinking that in other areas of his life he sure needed a map. She feigned irritation. "So what's so important that you had to drag me away from the party?"

"This." His hands circled her waist as he lowered his head to claim her lips in a kiss.

Through her foggy state, Casey thought she heard a twig snap. She playfully tapped his chest. "Your family isn't too far away."

"They can't see us," he said, trying to reclaim her lips.

She laughed. "So this is what you had in mind?"

He lounged back against a tree, his hands tight

around her waist as he settled her between his legs. She hooked her index fingers in his belt loops and swayed, his solid body her anchor.

"I wasn't about to come over while Ruby Sue bent your ear, but once she left, I couldn't help myself. Had to get you alone."

"I'm flattered."

"So, what did Ruby Sue want? Did she give you the third degree?"

"Actually, she wanted to know when we were getting hitched."

Ty's skin paled under his tan. "Come again?"

Casey felt his fingers relax around her waist and she clutched her fingers tighter through the loops, afraid he might lose his grip and send her sailing to the ground. "You heard me."

Ty blinked a few times.

"I'll give you a few minutes to get over the shock." She laughed at his poleaxed expression. "She caught me off guard too. I know how you feel."

"Why on earth did she ask you that?"

"She thinks you've got it bad for me."

"Oh." He looked pained. "Sorry. She's kinda . . . outspoken."

"I think your grandmother wants her family extended."

Ty leaned his head back against the tree trunk. Casey gave him a few minutes of silence to digest her information. "Your family is full of surprises."

"You don't know the half of it."

Casey reached over to brush Ty's hair from his forehead.

He stared into the woodland. A bird flapped overhead, flying into the horizon. Silence reigned. "You really want to get married?"

"Someday. With the right guy, of course."

"Casey . . ." he began, his tone laced with resignation.

"I know what you've told me," she quickly cut in, "but there will come a time when decisions have to be made for both of us."

"I know."

"You can't run from your past forever, Ty. If not me, what about the next woman?"

"Next woman?"

"At some point, a woman in your life will want to settle down. You're a good man, Ty. No woman would be able to keep from falling in love with you. But she won't wait indefinitely, and frankly, neither will I."

He brought his arm up and hooked it around her neck, drawing her head to rest on his shoulder. "The idea of loving again scares me," he whispered.

Casey embraced him, snuggling close. "Nothing is a sure thing, Ty. Not for any of us. We have to take chances in life, or life isn't worth living at all."

He didn't respond, but she took comfort in the steady rise and fall of his chest, the solid beat of his heart, and the fact that he stayed in her arms. She buried her nose in his shirt, drinking in his male scent.

She couldn't help it—she loved him. But saying those words aloud would only send him running. He wasn't ready yet.

And when he was, Casey hoped she'd be the

woman he chose to spend the rest of his life with. And she knew deep in her heart that she'd wait for him.

"Besides," she informed him, "I know a little something about taking risks. I took a big chance opening the store."

"We aren't talking about the store." Ty's muscles went rigid. Casey wondered if he considered the store competition, which was silly. The store was just a material possession. Granted, a big possession. But the time she'd spent with Ty and his family made her realize there was more to life. The store was like the icing on the cake.

Surely Ty understood that. Despite his apparent reluctance to discuss the store, she pressed on.

"Before the store, I'd always worked for someone else, always had the assurance that someone would take care of all the problems. But there aren't any sure things in life. You know that as well as I do. Don't you want to move on with your life?"

He shifted, bringing his hands to cup her face. Casey stood on her toes and kissed him, hoping all the love and tenderness she felt for him telegraphed into his soul.

The sound of scuffling leaves, along with muffled giggles, broke the kiss.

Casey spun around, squinting as she peered into the adjacent trees.

"I think we have company," Ty drawled. He stepped in front of her, his hands on his hips. "Okay, Emily. C'mon out."

The giggles erupted into full-blown laughter as Emily and her girlfriends scampered out of sight.

"I repeat," Casey said, shaking her head in amusement. "Your family is full of surprises."

Ty took her hand and they headed back to the party.

"When Ruby Sue hears about this, she'll never leave us alone."

Casey squeezed his hand. "That's fine with me."

"And about the future. . . ." he began, until the giggles echoed from another position, not as close by, but near enough to alert them that the girls were still on the prowl and could be within earshot.

"I think I need to have a talk with my niece."

Ty stalked off, leaving Casey to wonder what Ty planned for the future. And if he'd ever venture into this conversation again.

Chapter Ten

"Let's open presents," Emily yelled, as she and her friends scurried into the safety of the backyard. Casey couldn't blame her for the announcement. With Ty bearing down on the girls like an angry bear after its prey, she would have tried to draw the attention away from their impromptu spy mission, too.

Before Ty could reach Emily the family had gathered around the table, waiting for her to tear into her first present. He stopped just on the fringes of the group, but his eyes promised retribution. Emily had the good sense to keep her head down and stick to the job at hand.

Casey grinned at the scene before her, her senses going haywire when Ty came to stand close to her. His body warmth sent lacy tingles across her skin. After a few moments, he turned to her and winked. Casey smiled back. Of course he wasn't angry at Emily, but she knew he planned to play the game to the hilt.

His eyes darkened, and before she realized his intention, he had stepped behind her and circled his arms around her neck. Casey cupped her hands over his forearms. She loved the feel of him so close to her.

How drastically her life had changed in a matter of weeks. She'd gone from determined store owner and catalog entrepreneur who needed no one, to a woman deeply in love with a man she'd dreamed about since high school. It had happened so quickly, she had never even noticed the whirlwind until she was trapped in it.

But she wouldn't change the heady sensation for anything in the world.

Miles had been wrong. She didn't need the corporate world to fulfill her. This small Georgia community would not suffocate her. She felt more alive, more sure of her abilities and purpose in life than ever before.

Finally, Emily came to the last present. She read the card before removing the paper. "This is from Uncle Ty."

Casey turned her head in time to see Ty smile.

"You deserved the credit. After all, you did the shopping."

Emily opened the box, an exclamation of joy passing her lips. "This is sooo cool." She pulled out the clothing and held it up for all to see. After suitable expressions of envy from her friends, she ran to Ty.

He stepped away from Casey in time to catch his niece as she flung herself into his arms.

"Thank you," she said with the exuberance that comes with youth.

She gave him a peck on the cheek, then reached over and included Casey in the group hug. "Thanks for your present, too, Casey. You guys are the best."

"That's true," Ty told her, "but you're still in the doghouse."

Emily grinned unrepentantly. "Hey, I had to try."

Ty let her loose and she skipped back to the group surveying her gifts. The giggles returned in earnest.

Casey watched Ty as he grinned at the scene. "You make her happy."

He turned his mega-watt smile on her.

"Come and sing," Ruby Sue called, as she marched toward the table, carrying a birthday cake with burning candles.

The adults moved to the porch at the back of the house, waiting until the children finished eating before Ruby Sue brought more iced tea.

Ty noticed Gabe keeping a watchful eye over the guests, especially his wound-up daughter. On days like this, Gabe needed family. With Cindy's passing, he couldn't handle special days alone. And just like in the past, the family banded together in time of need.

A special pride welled in Ty. For Ruby Sue especially, and the years she'd dedicated to raising them. She'd done a good job, despite the obstacles.

Before long, evening descended with damp air settling around them. Parents arrived to take the girls home, leaving the family to sit around the porch table and share memories over coffee. Conversation for the Banner family took on a teasing edge as the siblings reminisced about the past. Ty sat close to Casey, grimacing when she heard the family secrets. He wondered why she didn't get up and run. Instead, she sat there, veiled in the flickering candlelight from the center of the table, a contented smile on her lips.

For once in his life, Ty appreciated who they were and where they'd come from. They had character, integrity. Always did. Despite what some people in town thought. And he realized any woman would be proud to be a part of this family. Especially Casey.

Emily skipped onto the porch and jumped into her father's lap. "Ready for bed?"

"Do I have to?"

"Yep. It's that time." Gabe hugged her tight. "Did you have a good time today, pumpkin?"

"Yes," she replied with a cheeky grin. "Especially when we caught Uncle Ty and Casey kissing in the woods."

Ty coughed out his iced tea. He glanced over to find Casey hiding her face in her hands.

Emily shot Ty a shrewd look, a mirror image of Ruby Sue. "Well, you were gonna tell on me anyway. I just beat you to it."

Gabe chuckled, then sobered. "Don't you know it's impolite to spy on people? Especially if they go into the woods? Alone?"

Emily picked at the hem of her nightgown. "We didn't know they were going there to kiss." Her pert nose wrinkled. "We just wanted to scare them."

"First rule of tailing," Ty advised. "Keep the giggles down to a dull roar."

"If you weren't kissing, we wouldn't have been laughing."

Ty raised an eyebrow at Gabe. "Is this the kind of child logic you have to live with?"

Gabe's lips tipped upward. "Every day."

"Man, you deserve a medal."

"I agree," he said in a pained voice. "Emily, tell Uncle Ty and Casey you're sorry and you won't do it again."

Emily slid off Gabe's lap and circled the table to stand before Ty. It took all his strength not to sweep her up in his arms.

"I'm sorry," she said solemnly. "And to you, too, Casey."

Casey reached out to brush a stray curl off Emily's forehead. "Apology accepted."

The girl's sober face softened to one of mischief. "Next time announce it when you want some privacy."

Before Ty could snatch her, Emily hightailed it into the house.

"I'll talk to her later." Gabe grimaced. "Mostly she's well behaved, but since Cindy's been gone, she has her moments. We're working on it."

Silence fell over the group, and Ty's heart went out to his brother. How would he feel if a woman he loved died? He didn't know if he could handle it like Gabe did. "Just remember, we're family. Any time you need us, call."

"We'll be there in a heartbeat," Marilyn added.

"Just like some other people I know," Gabe muttered, and winked at Casey.

She blushed, and deliberately avoided Ty's eyes.

"I remember the summer Ty graduated from high school." Gabe chuckled. "He was a bear to be around. Didn't you move away that year, Casey?"

She hesitated. "Yes."

"I guess that explains way he walked around in a funk."

"And his foul mood," Marilyn added.

Ty picked at the remainder of food on his plate. "Which is getting worse by the minute," he warned. "Don't y'all have anything better to talk about?"

"No." Marilyn and Gabe answered in unison.

"I didn't know you two dated," Marilyn said after a forkful of cake.

"We didn't exactly date," Casey corrected. "I helped him with a final report in school. We were friends."

"Still are." Ty's gaze met and held hers. He searched for a hidden meaning there, but she gazed down at her clasped hands.

"You mean he actually let you help him?" Gabe raised his eyebrows. "Wow. That's a first."

"You must have been special," Marilyn smiled directly at Casey. "He never did like us butting into his life."

"Still don't," came Ty's warning tone.

"And he never could take criticism," Ruby Sue groused as she joined them, the squeaky screen door slamming behind her. "Can't remember the amount of times I had to threaten to beat the boy before he'd listen up."

"What is this, rag-on-Ty night?" he asked.

Marilyn grinned. "Why not? You've done your share of beating on us."

Ty leaned back in the chair, lifting the front legs up as he tilted back to rest against the porch rail. "I think I've been pretty good to all of you."

Marilyn nodded. "Yeah, all things considered, you've been a great older brother."

Gabe lifted his coffee mug in salute. "That goes for me too."

Casey glanced at Ty with an I-told-you-so look. He chuckled, but didn't bother to hide his pleasure, flashing her a full-blown smile.

"He's still stubborn," Ruby Sue added, her gaze moving from Ty to Casey.

"I get it honestly," Ty teased back, still relishing his good humor.

Ruby Sue sighed. "This reminds me of old times, when you all were still living with me in the trailer. It's been too quiet now that Marilyn has her own place and Gabe's gone off to Florida with our Emily. Course, things have picked up a bit since Ty moved back."

They all laughed in agreement.

"This house is grand, but it gets a bit lonely."

Marilyn took her hand. "Gran, why didn't you say something?"

"You want me complaining like those old biddies down at the bingo hall?" She shook her head. "No ma'am, I'm thankful for my home. I just wish you were around more."

Ty saw varying degrees of guilt flash across all the faces around the table. Including his.

"Why don't you get a pet?" Casey asked.

Ruby Sue seemed surprised for a minute. "Never thought of that."

"I can get you a puppy from the pound," Gabe offered.

"No, don't want anything diggin' up my garden."

"That's right, you know how serious Ruby Sue is about her garden," Ty reminded them.

"How about a cat?" Gabe suggested. "Emily's been begging me for one. The two of you can go pick one out together."

Ruby Sue brightened. "Now that sounds like a good idea." She stood up, reaching across the table to remove plates. "Emily," she yelled, as she headed for the kitchen, "I got some good news for you."

Casey followed suit, clearing off the remaining dishes.

Ty grabbed her wrist. "You don't have to do that. You're a guest."

"It's okay. I want to."

He released her, watching her with hooded eyes as she cleaned up. For a gal who couldn't cook, she seemed so . . . domestic.

"Tyrone, where's your manners?" Ruby Sue yelled from the kitchen, her no-nonsense tone carrying through the screen door.

He stood, tapping Gabe on the arm. "Let's get outta here before Ruby Sue skins me alive."

Gabe pushed back his chair. "The girls left some games on the side of the house. Let's go pick up."

They walked around to the side of the house hidden in evening shadow. Bright light burned behind the curtains covering the windows.

"Casey looked perfectly happy to help clean up," Gabe remarked, sticking up for his older brother and his supposed lack of manners.

"She's polite to a fault."

"What does that mean? That she hasn't dumped you yet because you won't make a commitment?"

"Something like that."

"You're an idiot." Gabe spoke fervently.

Ty slid him a curious glance. "Really?"

Gabe hurled the ball he'd just picked up with a savage throw. "You have a fabulous girl who obviously adores you. She's right within your reach and you're too stubborn to grab hold of her and never let go."

Ty saw the pain in Gabe's eyes.

"I wish every day that Cindy was alive." He stopped abruptly, his voice thick with emotion.

"I'm sorry, Gabe."

"Don't let her go," his brother warned. "If you never listen to my advice again, at least believe me on this."

The night sounds clamored around them as the thick night air settled in. Light spilled from the window above them. Ty bent down to gather up the rings from a toss game. "I won't lie and say I understand your pain. I hope to God I never experience it."

"Don't say that. I wouldn't trade the time I had with Cindy for anything." Gabe retrieved the ball. "Since I've been home and seen how you and Marilyn are doing, I've come to the conclusion that I have to move on. Marilyn has to make a decision about her working all the time. And you have to make a decision about your life. Even if Casey's not the woman, you need to move on."

"She could be."

"Then give it a chance." Gabe's mood lightened. "Besides, I may ask her out if you don't make up your mind soon."

Ty didn't know what to say. Gabe asking Casey out? The idea didn't set well with him. But his brother was right about everything. The past wound him so tightly in its fist, he wasn't seeing things with Casey clearly. Maybe it was about time he started.

He began to reach for another ring when he noticed a loud, angry voice coming from the direction of the porch.

"Sounds like Marilyn," Gabe said.

"Let's go." Ty dropped the toys and jogged around the side of the house, Gabe on his heels. He reached the porch just as Casey stepped from the kitchen, concern etched on her lovely features.

Marilyn had the cell phone gripped in her hand so tightly that her knuckles were white. "I told you, I can't find the owner." A pause. "You can't take your business elsewhere. I'm the only Realtor who can help you. Hello? Hello?"

She slammed down the phone. "She hung up on me."

"Who?" Gabe asked.

Marilyn ran her hands through her sleekly styled hair, pulling until spikes of blond angled in her fingers. "A client. A very important client."

"Sabrina?" Ty asked.

All heads turned to him. Marilyn lowered her hands. "How did you know?"

"Look, if it'll stop this never-ending quest you're on, I'll get you to the owner."

"Who is it?" Marilyn asked, mirroring everyone's astonishment.

"Me."

Silence fell heavily around them. His gaze collided with Casey's.

Her eyes opened wide, first with shock, then hurt, and finally anger. He didn't blame her for her response. He had known she'd look at him this way. That was why he didn't tell her before now. He just never imagined she'd learn the truth under such heated circumstances.

Marilyn spoke first. "Since when?"

"Five years ago. When most of the stores were empty. Before interest returned to the square. I own most of the property." He ran a hand through his hair. "I incorporated so no one would know I was the owner. That's why you couldn't get to me. I deliberately stepped into the background and instructed my lawyers. They took care of the details."

"Sabrina doesn't know?" Gabe asked.

"No. Or she'd be all over me to sell."

"Why the secrecy?" Marilyn cried out.

He raked a hand through his hair. "It was best at the time."

"For who?" Casey asked, her thinly veiled anger piercing him.

"For me," he answered honestly.

Marilyn's voice grew shrill. "Do you mean to tell

me that all this time I've been searching for the owner and it was my own brother?"

"Guilty."

His sister's eyes glistened. "How could you do this to me? To my career?"

Ty sighed heavily. "This has nothing to do with your job. It was a business opportunity I invested in, for me. Nobody else."

"But all this time—" Marilyn started, before Ty cut in.

"All this time you've worked hard to make a name for yourself." He took a deep breath. "I know our childhood was hard. But we've grown up. Changed. Don't blame your problems on me or this situation, Marilyn. I never blamed you for Sabrina. Even though I knew why you wanted me to marry her."

Tears shimmered and leaked from Marilyn's eyes. "Ty is right. It was my . . . obsession to be someone that caused me to push Ty and Sabrina together. You may think my ambition seems selfish, but it's all I've got." Her voice dropped to a whisper. "I don't know what to do anymore."

Before Ty, or anyone else, could speak, Marilyn swept by Casey to enter the house.

"Uh, I think I'll go check on Emily." Gabe frowned at Ty. He passed by, halted beside Casey, and squeezed her shoulder. "Hear him out," he advised, then disappeared inside.

An uncomfortable silence enveloped Ty and Casey. For once in his life, Ty didn't know what to do, what to say to make things right.

He watched Casey hug her arms around her chest.

"Were you ever going to tell me?" she asked, her voice tight. "Or were you going to sell to that national chain that might destroy the town square?"

"I wouldn't do that."

"No? If I remember correctly, you told me it was only business."

"Things changed."

"Why?"

"You came back to town. Once I saw how important the store was to you, I didn't know what I should do. Sell or hold on."

"Are you saying you backed off for me?"

"Yes."

"Pardon me if I don't believe you," she scoffed. "You do just as you please, whenever you please. You had lots of opportunities to tell me the truth, but you never did. Sounds like you left yourself an out."

"I told you, some parts of my life I don't discuss."

"Save the rhetoric, Ty. You knew how concerned I was about my store but you never said a word."

"I knew I wasn't going to sell. You had nothing to worry about."

She opened her mouth in disbelief. Did his excuse sound that lame?

"But you never let me in on that little fact. You let me, and everyone else in town, worry about our future. How could you do that?"

"Maybe I'm tired of having to prove myself to everyone in this town," he lashed out. "I brought a lot of work here when those stores needed remodeling. And once we finished, the economy picked up. Nobody can complain about that. But Casey, I could never win around here. Nothing I did was ever good enough. People were mad if I stayed, mad if I left."

Casey gripped the back of the chair, but she couldn't hide her trembling. "So we should thank you for that? And forget all the worry of the last few weeks when one word from you would have changed everything?"

He cringed at her accusation. She was right. "Look, I made an error in judgement. Can't we just forget it and move on?"

"Oh, now you want to move on. Well, it's not so easy, Ty. I'll never know if one day you'll decide to leave town and sell the buildings when you go. You want me to trust you, but how do I know I can?"

"I wouldn't do that to you."

"Just like you never thought your fiancée would betray you?" Tears glittered in her eyes. "Now I know how you feel." She turned on her heel and slammed the screen door behind her.

Ty slumped against the porch post. What had he gotten himself into? He never meant to hurt anyone. It was his investment, meant for him alone. He'd never planned to share the information and one day, when he left, he would take the money with him.

But so much had changed. Casey had captured his heart, and now he had lost her. He came back full circle, back to the same place he was before.

Alone.

He could blame Casey for barging into his life and giving him hope again, but he was honest enough to admit he'd created his own self-fulfilling prophecy.

He had no one to blame but himself.

* * *

Casey sat on the front porch swing, waiting for Marilyn to take her home. She rocked, numb to anything but the hurt of Ty's betrayal. Why hadn't he ever confided in her? He'd had plenty of opportunity.

The front door opened and Emily slipped out, her small feet shuffling over the painted wood. She climbed up on the swing beside Casey, pulling her nightgown securely around her.

"I came to say good night and to thank you for coming to my party."

Casey reached over and tucked Emily in her embrace. "I was glad to come," she said.

They swung together, watching fireflies dart in the darkness, as Emily's warmth eased Casey's coldness.

"I miss my mom," Emily confided.

"I miss my mom, too," Casey admitted, wishing she could run home to the security of a mother's loving arms.

"Is your mom dead?"

Casey brushed her cheek over Emily's downy soft hair. "No, but she never wanted to be around me much."

"My mom loved to do stuff with me."

Casey squeezed her. "She sounds special."

"She was. When she got sick, she made me promise that I'd pray for someone to love daddy after she went away." Emily gazed up into Casey's face. "If you weren't Uncle Ty's girlfriend, I'd have wished for you."

Casey blinked back the agonizing tears of gratitude. "Thank you," she whispered.

The swing creaked as Casey held Emily close. Holding the young girl, who had lost her mother at such a young age, kept her from concentrating on her own broken heart.

Chapter Eleven

Casey holed up in her house for two days before she had the strength to venture back into the real world. She'd spent the previous days productively, adding the final touches to the catalog and website. The mail order business was officially ready to roll.

She'd kept her mind busy so she wouldn't dwell on Ty. Unfortunately, she'd been a complete failure in that regard.

Wandering into the kitchen, she made a pot of coffee, then took a pad and pencil to make a list of her errands: bring proofs to the printer; check on inventory at the store; go to the post office; don't think about Ty.

Don't think about Ty.

After pouring a steaming cup, she peered out the window. The driveway was empty. She'd hoped to see the battered pickup. Did she really expect him to show up for work? Especially after the bombshell he dropped?

Trying to ignore the questions circling her mind, she concentrated on the hot brew on her tongue, the hunger pangs in her stomach.

But still she wondered where he was. What he was doing.

"Stop it," she muttered out loud. He'd made his decisions and he had to live with them.

Just as she had to.

But just the same, hurt assailed her. Why hadn't he just told her the truth about his owning the buildings? What possible difference would it have made? It all went back to his wanting a friendly relationship with her, but not sharing his heart. And to her, sharing meant sharing *everything* in his life.

That's what hurt the most. With Miles, she'd known from the start that he wanted to move up the ladder—that he'd knock down whoever got in his way in his quest to make it big. Including her. But Ty was different.

Or at least she thought he was.

Disgusted with her relentless train of thought, she dumped the coffee down the drain and ran upstairs to dress for the day.

Thirty minutes later she entered Crafty Creations. "Hey, Bonnie."

Her cousin met her with a beaming smile. "Heard the good news yet?"

"I just got here."

Bonnie could barely contain her excitement. "We're saved. Ben and Molly called from the General Store to break the news. The owner isn't going to sell. In fact, he's offered every store owner a chance to buy him out."

Casey found the nearest chair and plopped herself down. "All this happened today?"

"Yep. You may want to go see Marilyn. She's handling the details."

"I'll do that."

"You okay?" Bonnie asked, noticing Casey's stunned reaction for the first time.

"Yeah," she answered, distracted by the current news. "Do you know the identity of the owner?"

"No. Does it matter?" Bonnie broke into an impromptu jig. "He wants to sell."

Casey stood, a flush of indignation sweeping through her. Did Ty think that just because he offered to sell that everything would be all right? That he could change the fact that he hadn't been up-front and honest with her? What was he trying to prove?

She abruptly left Bonnie and walked the block to the real estate office. Marilyn sat poised behind her desk, the phone wedged between her ear and neck as she carried on a conversation and fished through papers scattered across the desktop.

"I'll get the contract out just as soon as possible. Yes, today if you need it." She hung up and sighed. "What a day."

"So I've heard."

"Bonnie told you?" Marilyn asked, her tone uneasy.

"Yes. What's going on?"

Marilyn leaned back in her high-back leather chair. "Ty wants to sell."

"Why now?"

"He didn't give me any details, just asked me to handle the sale."

"And you don't have a problem with that?"

She shrugged. "Why should I? It's legitimate and it's what he wants."

"Ty doesn't know what he wants."

"That may be true in his personal dealings, but in this he was very precise. He only asked that, for now, I keep his name out of any transactions."

"Can he do that?" Casey scowled at Marilyn. "What's he up to?"

A frown of worry marred Marilyn's forehead. "He can do anything he wants, and I don't know what he's up to. He called me the day after Emily's party with his plans. I haven't heard from him since. Gran says he hasn't been to the trailer." She glanced up at Casey. "How about you? Have you seen him?"

"No. And I don't expect to."

"You mean he's finished the work at your place?"

Casey vaguely shook her head, concerned over the increasing frown on Marilyn's face. She hated the sinking feeling in her stomach, the need to know if Ty was okay. Her mind logically reminded her that she was angry with him, but her heart had a way of challenging her logic. "I'm sure he's fine," she tried to reassure Marilyn, as well as herself. "There's no need to worry."

Marilyn gathered her papers together in a neat pile. "But it's not like him to take off without telling one of us. Even when he left Sabrina he called us to say where he was. This time, nothing."

"Maybe he wants to be alone."

"Even if he didn't admit his ownership and have us all upset, this is a bad time for him. He needs family, even when we want to ring his neck."

"Why?"

The phone rang. "Look, now isn't a good time. I'll have to get back to you."

Casey stood her ground. Now was not the time for Marilyn's evasive tactics. She'd wait for Marilyn to finish the call, then demand answers. She wasn't going to leave without the truth, or her chance to buy the store. Coming up with the money would be a problem, but she'd figure out a way.

Marilyn replaced the receiver, digging through the stack she'd just made.

"What do I need to do to buy the store?" Casey asked.

A flush covered Marilyn's cheeks. "There's nothing you can do. The only store not for sale is yours."

Casey's breath left her in one fell swoop. It took a few seconds to speak. "What? That's not fair."

Marilyn held up her hands, clearly uncomfortable imparting this information. "I don't know why. He didn't say and I didn't ask."

"Why didn't you ask? You know how much I have at stake in this." An unwelcome thought came to mind. "What about Sabrina? Is he willing to sell to her?" she asked sharply.

"Let's just say we're keeping the information quiet until the final transactions." Marilyn's expression softened. "Casey, he's my brother. And he's right. I owe him. I have to go by his wishes."

As if that excused everything.

Sick to her stomach, Casey backed out of the office. In a daze, she stumbled to a shaded bench in the court square, confusing thoughts bombarding her. The traffic became a dull sound and tourists' voices grew dim as she focused on a plan of action.

She had to find Ty and ask him, no, beg him if she had to, to sell her the store. That old familiar feeling of depending on someone else, only to have them pull the rug out from under her, reared its ugly head again. Ty knew how much this success meant to her, *why* would he deliberately sabotage her? Had she pushed him too far in admitting how much she wanted a permanent relationship with him?

Questions rushed through her mind, but the only answers she needed were from Ty himself.

Driving around Paineville searching for Ty had proven fruitless. He wasn't at his usual haunts, and no one had seen him. Mike Post had gone back home, so she couldn't ask him for help. That left only one person.

Ruby Sue was rocking back and forth on the porch when Casey ventured up to the house. Hesitating on the stairs, Casey's heart ached at the worry etched on the woman's face.

"Been expectin' you."

"Do you know where he is?" Casey asked.

"Haven't seen the boy. I checked the trailer out back in the woods. Nothing. He might have gone off by himself to figure things out."

"Marilyn says he doesn't go anywhere without telling someone."

"This time is different."

"Why?" Casey blurted, remembering how Marilyn had hinted the same way. "What's going on?"

"It's been a year to the day that Sabrina broke the engagement."

The sudden realization struck her. So that explained the family rallying around him. On such an emotional day, they'd be there for support and love. No matter what he'd done. Or who he'd done it to.

She felt sick.

Ruby Sue motioned for Casey to join her on the swing. "He wanted to sell that property about three years ago. I talked him out of it. Kept telling him it was better that someone who loved this town keep hold of those buildings until times got better. So he held on."

"I never got the impression he loved this town."

"He doesn't let on." Ruby Sue chuckled. "He was miserable when he moved to the city. Not just because of Sabrina, they were all but over anyway. No, he missed the mountains. Knowing that those who really love him are here. He was born here, and like most folks around, he'll die here."

"Then where do you think he is?"

"Been tryin' to think of places he liked to go, but nothing comes to mind. Course, he was secretive as a child. Still is. Guess that's the way he protects himself."

Casey hesitated to bring up the past, but she found

herself curious about things Ty would never tell her. "His mother really did a number on him."

Ruby Sue rocked. "Yes, she did. Ty loved her, but that wasn't enough to keep her here. She never did have much use for the country, was always looking to get out. And one day she did. From that day on Ty became the head of the family. Just came to him naturally."

"And then Sabrina left him."

"That wasn't much to cry over, but it did knock him silly." Her keen eyes captured Casey's. "All the women he's loved in his life have left him and he's had no control. For a man with his kind of pride, it hits deep and stays there."

"You've always been there for him. The one true constant in his life."

She nodded, her voice thick. "I'm proud of that boy."

"But that doesn't excuse what he did. He hid the truth from me."

"When it comes to you, the boy doesn't think straight."

"I wish that were a compliment."

Ruby Sue grinned and swiped at her eyes. "It is."

"I don't want him to leave me."

"Have you told him that?"

"He hasn't asked how I feel."

"He won't."

The afternoon sun warmed the porch, birds sang in the distant treetops. Casey gazed over the grassy landscape. The trailer was hidden in the woods, out of eyesight. Not that it mattered. Ty wasn't there.

"What could be worse than Ty not telling you about those buildings?" Ruby Sue asked.

"Him not loving me." The words tumbled from her lips.

"Is that what you're really all riled up about?"

Was it? If Casey was honest with herself she'd have to admit the truth. And the truth was that it was easier to be angry over Ty's actions than to face the fact that he wouldn't commit to her. That he didn't want a future with her. That she was so in love with him that she ached to her bones.

"I can deal with his past disappointments. I can even forgive him for not telling me he owns my store. But if he can't say the words, then I can't give him my heart. No matter how much I love him."

Ruby Sue nodded, great sadness reflected in her eyes.

There was nothing more to say.

"I need to get back to the store," Casey said, as she rose from the swing.

"Want me to let you know when he gets back?"

"I want him to come on his own with no bullying from you."

A grin. "Girl after my own heart."

Casey woke with a sudden start. She rolled to her side and glanced at the clock. Midnight. Moonlight poured through the open window.

Bunching the pillow, she laid back and stared at the ceiling. The creak and groans of the settling foundation serenaded her. Vaguely she remembered having a dream. The elusive quality clouded her understanding.

But a startling urgency stayed with Casey, unsettling her spirit.

A crunching sound, like footsteps on gravel, jolted her to attention. She sat up, straining to hear the sound again. Was it her imagination? Seconds later she heard it again.

Jumping from the bed, she eased to the window and drew back the curtains a fraction, peeking outside. She glimpsed a shadowy figure moving down the driveway.

Panic seized her. Was someone prowling around her house?

Another sound drew her attention to the backyard. In the stream of moonlight she spied the gazebo. It looked normal at first glance, until she noticed a pair of crossed boots illuminated in the light's path. She squinted, hoping to get a better view. As she scanned the darkened interior, she saw the shadow of a man. And then recognition struck.

Ty.

Caught between elation and fear, Casey grabbed an old quilt from the back of a chair and wrapped it around her cotton nightgown. She hurried down the stairs, through the house, and out into the night. The dew tickled her toes as she ran through the grass. By the time she reached the steps to the gazebo, her breathing came hard.

Ty had never seen such a welcoming sight. His own angel: her hair wild around her face, her eyes bright with anticipation.

He swallowed hard.

He must have been crazy to come here.

But it was the only place he wanted to be.

"Ty?" she questioned. "What on earth are you doing here?"

He combed a hand through his damp hair, trying to put the right words to his actions. "I wanted to see you, Casey. I wanted to explain."

"No more excuses?"

"No. The truth."

She sat beside him on the edge of the bench, allowing a small space between them.

He took a labored breath. "I never meant to deceive you. My intention had always been to someday sell that property. To take that nest egg and start up somewhere new. Somewhere far from here.

"But when Sabrina came nosing around, I finally had leverage over her I didn't have before. I enjoyed playing the cat-and-mouse game with her. For once I had the advantage. Can't say I'm proud of it."

He tried to gauge her reaction but her eyes were shadowed by the darkness. "By then you'd come into my life and I'd decided not to sell. But I still didn't want Sabrina to find out about the ownership, so I kept my mouth shut. I felt guilty about that, and I realize now that I should have told you."

"I wouldn't have told anyone."

"Deep down I knew that, but by telling you, I had to admit that what we have is important." His voice grew thick. "So much has happened and you being in my life again . . . it caught me off guard."

She didn't seem surprised. "I never meant to push you, Ty."

He pinched the bridge of his nose. "You didn't. I was already falling for you."

Her eyebrows rose.

"I know I haven't made things easy for you," he admitted.

"True. But I guess I understand."

"Do you?" he asked, surprised by her calmness when he expected righteous anger.

"Sure." She took his hand and gently stroked it. "And I'll never leave you. Not ever."

"Not unless I push you away."

"What do you mean?" she asked, surprise in her expression.

"Face it, Casey, I'm not an easy man to deal with. Just look at where I came from."

"Do you really think that's true? Ty, your mother abandoned you. No woman who really cares about her children could do a thing like that. And as for Sabrina, I think her actions speak for themselves."

He closed his eyes, unwilling to endure Casey's compelling features as she tried to reason with him.

She continued. "And what kind of woman wants material things over a man's love?"

"That was the problem. Deep down I think Sabrina knew my love for her had faded. Maybe even before I did. I went through the motions, tried to believe I cared. But we'd both changed. So you see, it's really my fault she left."

Casey laced her fingers with his.

"A year ago today she left me. She's moved on and I'm in the same rut, allowing bitterness to hold me back."

Cradling his face with her hands, Casey gazed into his eyes. Her features softened. "You have the power to change that."

"How?"

"With my help."

"Why would you want to? I made it clear from the start that I didn't want you involved in my life. God, what a fool I've been. You must hate me."

"Hardly," she answered in a strangled voice.

"I drove Sabrina away. I'll do the same to you."

"You don't give me much credit." To his surprise, Casey covered his mouth with hers. Her soft lips melded with his, providing immediate comfort until he broke contact.

"I don't want to get in the way of your future. Your happiness. Casey, I know that store means everything to you. You've worked hard to make it a success."

"Success is fine, unless you don't have someone special to share it with. It could never take the place of building a relationship. Building a family."

"You don't know how glad I am to hear you say that."

"The store is important to me. But so are you, Ty."

"I guess I made up all this competition in my head."

Casey smiled. "I understood why you felt that way. But the past is over. We both want the same thing. Don't we?"

"Yeah. I think we do."

"Business and personal lives separate?"

"Okay."

"Then will you sell the building to me?"

"You spoke to Marilyn already?"

"When I went to work Bonnie gave me the good news. It was good news, until I found out I'm the only tenant you wouldn't consider selling to."

"I have a good reason."

"Which is?"

He pulled a folded paper from the pocket of his denim shirt. "I want to give you the property. No money needs to be exchanged, no strings attached."

He held out the deed his attorney had drawn up.

She frowned at it. "Why the special treatment?"

"Because of what we have."

Her gaze traveled from the paper to meet his. "What we have?"

He tucked her hair behind her ear. "I haven't felt this way in a lot of years, Casey. I need you."

"For how long?"

"I don't know," he told her honestly. "I'm afraid to make the step. To promise forever."

"I need to hear those promises, Ty, otherwise I can't accept this." She nodded toward the paper in his hand. "I'll come up with the money, just like everyone else. I don't want to be singled out because of our so-called friendship. That wouldn't be fair to Ben and Molly, who consider you family. Or May at the diner, or anyone. I won't take it."

He shook his head, thinking he hadn't heard her right. "I'm still not gettin' this right. Let me get this straight. You're turning me down?"

"Under the current conditions, yes."

"That's crazy. I've just offered you security."

"No, I think you're trying to ease your conscience."

"Well, whatever my motive is, I still want you to take my offer."

She stood, clutching the quilt tighter and higher around her neck. "And I refuse. I've made it this long on my own. I'll be fine."

"Is your independence so important to you that you won't give in?"

"It's more than just my independence. It's about your true feelings for me. If you can't come right out and tell me how you feel, then there's no deal."

Ty pushed himself up, reaching out to rest his hand against the gazebo door post. "I thought you weren't going to push me."

"I'm not."

"Well this sure feels like a corner to me."

"If that's how you feel, then you can't see what I have to offer."

"And what's that?"

"You want to hear the words out loud? Okay." She held up her hand and counted off the fingers as she made her point. "A woman who won't run away from you. Who will be there in good times and bad. A woman you can trust." She took a ragged breath. "A woman who loves you."

Ty closed his eyes. Deep in his gut he knew how she felt.

"Then help me, Casey. Help me forget the past and just love me."

Time suspended. His chest tightened as he strained to hear her next words. Blood roared through his veins in anticipation.

He barely heard her when she spoke, her voice as

soft as gossamer wings. "You have to take the first step. I can't do it for you. You have to change your circumstances, Ty. Then we can be together."

"And will you be here when I get this mess with the business under control? No matter how long it takes?"

"Yes."

He saw the promise in her eyes and his heart melted. "Then that's what I'll do."

Chapter Twelve

"Where are you off to in such a hurry?" Bonnie asked before Casey shrugged on her jacket. "We have to unload the shipment."

"Molly said she'd take some time off from the General Store and help you. I have my cooking lesson."

"Geez. Three months and you'd think you'd get the hang of it by now."

"Hey, I'm a slow burner, I mean learner. Bye."

Casey stepped into the crisp autumn afternoon and headed for her SUV. She really was getting the hang of cooking, even though Bonnie thought otherwise.

In truth, she really enjoyed the time she spent with Ruby Sue. She had become the mother that Casey had always dreamed about. After getting through her rough exterior, Casey discovered a warm heart, ready to love at a moment's notice.

No wonder Ty and his siblings had grown up so

well. Ruby Sue poured herself into their lives and now she reaped the reward.

Ty had left town the morning after his announcement in the gazebo. He meant to keep his word and work through his problems. But she hadn't heard from him since. This had been the longest three months of her life. She wondered what Ty was doing. Did he miss her as much as she missed him? This state of limbo brought out her insecurities, all her fears. Was he so busy he couldn't call and ease her mind?

She refused to ask Ruby Sue, who had heard from her grandson. Frustration roared through her. She thought they'd made a major step in their relationship.

Instead, he'd left her behind.

He sent a couple of men to finish the barn and she was filling it with merchandise daily. The website was a success. The catalog sales were booming.

If only she could boast the same for herself.

She spent the ten-minute drive to Ruby Sue's trying not to dwell on the failed romance. Of course, she could hardly avoid it since she was the gossip of the town. Ironic, how she'd tried to avoid it, but once again others knew about her problems. Or thought they knew.

But Casey focused on the fact that she'd given her heart to a man she loved. With so much pain and suffering in the world, Casey believed that giving love, even if not returned, was all anyone could ask for.

Ruby Sue met her on the steps to the porch. "Your cousin give you a hard time about leaving the store today?"

"Yes. How'd you know?"

"She called here to see if you'd arrived yet."

"Is something wrong?"

"Not at all," Ruby Sue smiled, mischief twinkling in her eyes.

"Well, let's get started." Casey hooked her arm through the older woman's and headed into the warm house. "I'm determined to beat you in the pie contest next summer."

"Honey, you and the entire town." Ruby winked. "But it's never gonna happen."

"We'll see."

The phone rang a few minutes later and while Ruby Sue took the call, Casey readied the ingredients for the pies.

"That was Gabe. He's bringing Emily home for Thanksgiving. Sounded like he might be planning on stayin'."

Casey hugged her. "That's wonderful. I know how much that means to you."

"We didn't have much when the kids were growin' up, but we were together. We had turkey and my special pies."

"Maybe I could take over pie duty this year. Start a new tradition."

Ruby Sue narrowed her eyes. "You think you can handle it?"

"I have to start somewhere."

The older woman nodded. "Okay. You get busy and I'll plan the dinner." She fished through the roll-top desk in the corner of the room for paper and a pen. "If only I could have my entire brood home. . . ." Her eyes flashed in a moment of irritation.

"He'll be back when he's ready."

"Foolish boy. He's been gone long enough."

"If there's one thing I've learned, it's that you can't force Ty." She didn't want to think about his absence. It still felt like an exposed wound open to the air. She figured someday it would heal. "Now, about these winning pies."

Despite her claim to secrecy, Ruby Sue revealed why no one made a pie as good as hers. "When someone asks, I always make sure I leave out a little something in my recipe. That's why not one woman in this town can figure out why theirs don't taste as good as mine." A broad smile flashed across Ruby Sue's lips. "But I gotta special place for you in my heart and I'm gonna share my secret. Wait while I go fetch my special spices." She pulled her apron over her head and opened the back door. "I'll be right back," she called behind her.

Casey grinned and poured more filling into the crust, managing to drop a glob right onto the side of her sneaker. She looked down in time to see the gooey mixture stream into her shoe. "Oh, for Pete's sake" she muttered, grabbing a towel to clean up the mess.

Casey looked at the sad condition of her flour-dusted clothes and laughed. "No one ever told me kitchen work was such a messy job." She bent down to untie the laces, then slipped out of her sneakers.

She started down the hallway to the bathroom and froze in her tracks. Ty stood at the other end of the hall, his gaze piercing hers. He looked wonderful, his broad shoulders clad in flannel, filling the breadth of the doorway.

After months of mental rehearsal, she couldn't think of a word to say. Especially as he closed the distance between them. A grin tugged at his lips as he visually took in her bare feet. Adorned with bright red polish. "Girl, you always know how to get to me."

Grazing his knuckle over her cheek, he removed a smudge of crust. "I see you've been busy since I've been gone."

She stepped back, fearing her reaction to his nearness. Instead, she kept the conversation light. "Yeah, well Ruby Sue told me the only real way to catch a man is through his stomach. So she's teaching me the ropes."

"I always said Ruby Sue talks too much." Sensing her dread, he allowed her a hairsbreadth of space.

"Maybe so, but I can cook now."

"No more frozen dinners?"

"Not in this lifetime."

"What else don't you want in this lifetime?"

"To be alone," she whispered.

"Maybe I could solve that."

When she didn't answer, he lowered his head and drew her into his kiss. Casey clasped the front of his flannel shirt, drinking in the outdoorsy scent of him and the heat of his large body so close to hers.

It was as if no time at all had passed between them.

With trepidation, Casey broke the kiss and took a step back, waiting for the bomb to drop. "Why are you here, Ty?"

"Home for the holidays."

"That's it?"

"And to check up on my investments." He leaned

against the wall, casually crossing his arms over his chest. "You didn't have to buy the store, Casey."

She lifted her chin. "Yes, I did."

He let out a long-suffering sigh. "Well, you ruined the plan."

"What plan?"

"I planned on giving you the entire vacant building in the square. So you could move the store and keep your inventory and mail-order business under one roof."

She didn't bother hiding her shock. "Give me the building?"

"Yep. With only one string attached."

She frowned. *Here it comes.* "What?"

"That you marry me."

The breath left her body and her eyes opened wide. She finally inhaled enough air to speak. "Repeat that."

"You heard me." He took her hand and she slithered back along the wall, trying to keep a sensible distance from him. He grinned. "Hey, I'm cornering *you* for a change."

"Just explain," she squeaked out. This was torture, pure torture.

"I went to Atlanta and sold my half of the business. You're right, Casey, I don't need the past holding me back. I realized I want all the things you want: a loving wife and a houseful of kids. But you were right. I had to take that first step. Once I sold the partnership, I set my other priorities in place. I'm only sorry it took so long."

"Why didn't you call me?"

"I knew the second I heard your voice over the

phone I'd drop everything and hightail it home. But I had to finish the past, make sure it was all gone before coming home to my future."

He paused for a minute.

"I love you, Casey. Forever. And that's a promise I'm willing to keep."

Her heart pounded at his words. She stared at him—a man she never thought would admit those words to her—and tried to make sense of the whole thing.

Concern filled his eyes when she was silent for so long. "So? What's your answer?"

"I think it's too late."

His eyebrows rose as his face paled. "Don't say that, Casey. Give me a chance. I know it took me a while to realize what I was missing, but I'm 100 percent sure now. I want you—need you—in my life. Permanently and with no strings attached."

She watched him carefully, but could only see complete honesty on his face.

"No more leaving me out of decisions?"

"No."

"No more leaving without telling me where you're going?"

He shook his head fervently. "No way."

"No more living in the past?"

"I've done that and it brought me nothing but loneliness. I want you, kids, the whole works." He swallowed. "What do you say?"

She cast aside old doubts and clung to the vision of their future together. "I say, yes. To everything."

Ty let out a loud whoop, gathering her in his arms and twirling her around. His lips settled over hers in a long, promising seal until Casey broke the kiss to draw in much-needed air.

Ty lowered her to the floor, but kept her in his firm embrace. She hugged his waist and rested her head on his shirt, determined never to let him go again. From now on, she'd make sure they were always together, in mind and in heart.

Her dreams had come true. For now. For always.

A lasting love.